FOWL PLAY, DESDEMONA

FOWL PLAY, DESDEMONA

BY BEVERLY KELLER

LOTIIROP, LEE & SHEPARD BOOKS   NEW YORK

First Edition 1 2 3 4 5 6 7 8 9 10

Library of Congress Cataloging in Publication Data
Keller, Beverly. Fowl Play, Desdemona by Beverly Keller.
    p.   cm. Summary: Dez teams up with Sherman, a vegetarian and animal
rights activist, to design posters for the school play with humorous results.
ISBN 0-688-06920-7 [1. Single-parent family—Fiction.   2. Animals—Treatment—
    Fiction.]   I. Title. PZ7.K2813Dd   1989   [Fic]—dc19   88-9481 CIP AC

For Bertha Gilbert

One

Monday of the week before Thanksgiving, Sherman Grove, our landlord's son, arrived at our back door as usual to walk Antony and me to school. My brother Antony was in the morning kindergarten session and my sister Aida in the afternoon, so I walked Antony to school and Aida home.

Neither Sherman nor my brother nor I said anything for the first block.

I was worrying about Thanksgiving. When you live with only one parent, holidays can be a hard mixture of celebration and emptiness. My father hadn't said what we were going to do. Since Mrs. Farisee, our housekeeper, would surely have the day off, I figured it was a choice between my father and me making dinner, or taking the twins to some restaurant. Either seemed so depressing, I couldn't bring myself to ask him.

Still, I was so uncomfortable about the holiday I

had to bring it up now, like scratching a mosquito bite.

"So what are you doing for Thanksgiving?" I asked Sherman.

"What do you mean, what am I doing?" he demanded.

"Are you having dinner at home?"

"Sure. You think my family is shipping me somewhere for the occasion? You think I'm going hang gliding or something?"

I should have wondered why he was so touchy, but I was feeling edgy myself. "Boy. You know, just walking to school with older guys, Sherman, you're getting obnoxious."

"Now you're saying Mike Harbinger is obnoxious?" he demanded.

"No. That's what's interesting. Neither he nor his friends are, which makes me wonder how they can stand you."

Antony looked from me to Sherman anxiously. "What are you guys fighting about?"

"I asked him what he was going to do for Thanksgiving," I told Antony, "and he took it as a personal insult."

"Hey, Antony!" Mike Harbinger's little brother Preston came barreling toward us from a side street, along with a gaggle of other kindergartners. Preston was the first friend my brother had ever had. Before that, Antony was content just to socialize with Aida.

2

Mike and some other high school stars were right behind Preston.

It's strange how your life can suddenly change, and then within a few days you begin to take the change for granted. At the beginning of the semester, I was just some new girl in junior high. Nobody cared where I came from, or even talked to me, except for Sherman.

Then my brother made friends with Preston, and Mike Harbinger and his friends started walking with us on their way to school. Any girl in junior high, probably even high school, would have given away her whole sweater collection just to have Mike *speak* to her.

Suddenly, almost everybody in my class became my instant close friend. Marti Dunnigan and Kerri White and Teena Brannigan and Laurelle Carson, the most popular girls in my school, even begged their parents to let them get a haircut like mine.

Not that Mike or his friends paid much attention to me. They talked about football and music videos and cars and high-tech stuff. This is where Sherman could hold his own. He's a genius when it comes to computers and the like.

This morning, though, Sherman was left out. Mike was turning sixteen on Friday. His mother was going to pick him up after school and take him down to the DMV to get his driver's license. So the big question was whether his folks would let him have one of their cars Saturday to take his friends to a drive-in.

There was really nothing for Sherman or me to say. Thinking of Mike driving around in a car, I suddenly realized he'd be *voting* in two more years, and Sherman and I would still be a couple of kids.

Preston and the kindergartners with him were going on about Thanksgiving, in a kind of counterpoint to Mike and his friends talking about driving and licenses.

"We're going to have the biggest turkey we've *ever* had," Preston announced. "And all my aunts and uncles and their kids are coming over. . . ."

"We're going to my grandmother's," another little boy declared. "And we'll probably have two kinds of pies and get tons of leftovers to take home."

My brother didn't say anything.

We dropped Antony and Preston and the other kindergartners at the grade school, Mike and I cautioning our brothers to come directly home. Then Sherman and I walked on to junior high, and Mike and his friends walked on to their high school.

At least they hadn't talked about any plans for Mike's birthday party. Naturally, he couldn't invite an eleven-and-a-half-year-old boy and a twelve-and-a-half-year-old girl, and he was too nice a person to talk about it in front of us.

When I got to my locker, Marti Dunnigan, Kerri White, and Laurelle Carson were already there, trying to console Teena Brannigan.

Teena had the lead in *The King and I,* our school's first play of the year, and both Marti and Kerri had speaking parts. This was to be expected, I thought. You could guarantee that Marti and Kerri would be pom-pom girls and cheerleaders in high school.

Teena was taller than either of them, with long black hair and dark eyes, and she even dressed a little more far-out. You could just bet she would write poetry for the high school newspaper.

The closer it got to the opening of *The King and I,* the more Teena and Marti and Kerri acted as if this were the biggest event since the dawn of man.

The performances were originally supposed to be on the Friday and Saturday nights before Thanksgiving. But Mr. Razi, the director, got sick, and so the play had to be postponed until the Saturday and Sunday after Thanksgiving.

That meant three kids had already had to drop out of the chorus because their parents were taking them out of town for the holiday.

Mr. Razi stood fast, though. He maintained that if he gave the cast three days off without rehearsals, they'd forget their lines and have to start all over, so they probably wouldn't be ready by Christmas.

Since I had nothing to do with the play, I could see both sides. But I had a feeling that, to Teena and Marti and Kerri, Thanksgiving was just something that interfered with *The King and I.* They might even be insulted if I asked them what they were doing for the holiday.

Kerri and Marti and Laurelle were in a cluster around Teena, who was talking fast and low and hard, her back against her locker.

"What happened?" I asked.

"Lars Svenson," Laurelle told me. "He says he won't shave his head."

Mr. Razi had cast Lars Svenson to play the King of Siam, though Lars was a blond with light blue eyes and pale eyelashes and eyebrows. He was the only junior high boy who not only was taller than Teena, but also had a lower voice.

"It should be a *requirement*," Teena said. "Razi should have asked every kid who showed up for tryouts if he was willing to shave his head to be the king."

"You'd need parents' permission, too," Laurelle murmured. "In writing."

I couldn't tell whether she was serious or not. Laurelle had tried out for *The King and I*, but didn't get even a part in the chorus.

In junior high, of course, a director can't leave anybody out, so Mr. Razi put Laurelle on stage crew.

She got kicked off almost at once.

Mr. Hofstaeder, the custodian, who was in charge of stage crew, gilded a chair for the King of Siam's throne. Laurelle sat in it, and then said that it was his fault for not putting a Wet Paint sign on it and that he should pay for ruining her good skirt and sweater.

Mr. Hofstaeder has a horrible temper. So Laurelle was put on the makeup crew.

So she wasn't really *in* the play, and she didn't seem to feel as involved as Teena and Marti and Kerri.

"I'm just not willing to go through with it." Teena shook her head a little harder than I thought was necessary.

"Of course, it doesn't say anywhere in the play that the king is bald," Kerri pointed out.

"Everybody *knows* he's bald!" Teena cried.

"No." For once I could say something about the play. "Everybody knows that Yul Brynner was bald in the movie. That doesn't mean . . ."

Nobody even looked at me.

"It's bad enough that I've got to play opposite a blue-eyed kid who's supposed to be the King of Siam," Teena declared. "But I will not, I will absolutely not, play opposite a blond King of Siam. The minute he steps onstage, the whole audience will break up."

"Not if they don't know where Siam is," Kerri said.

"Where is Siam, anyway?" Laurelle wondered.

Teena looked like somebody yelling "Fire!" in a house full of people busy ignoring her.

"Maybe you could wrap Lars's head in a turban," Kerri mused.

"They don't *wear* turbans in Siam!" Teena snapped.

"How do you know, if you've never been there?" Kerri demanded.

"It's called Thailand now," Sherman said. "It's between Laos and Cambodia."

Nobody even said oh.

Except for Mike and his friends, few people do listen to Sherman. Of course, Sherman is not in the mainstream of American childhood. He is, in fact, your classic wimp—undersize and pale, wispy, and unaggressive.

He is also a library of information most people don't care much about.

For instance: Crocodiles take the most tender care of their hatchlings.

For instance: Rupert Sheldrake, a director of biochemistry at Cambridge University, wrote *A New Science of Life.* So? you ask. Well, when he was working with rats, Sheldrake found that if one rat in one place learns something, other rats, thousands of miles away, without ever meeting that rat, or having that experience, learn the same thing without being taught.

"Somebody is just going to have to tell Lars . . ." Teena began, when Faye Brower joined us.

Faye didn't get a part in the play either, so Mr. Razi put her on the publicity committee.

"Guess what! My big sister's getting *married*!" Faye announced. "*And* . . ." She paused dramatically. "She's giving me her drum majorette outfit, *plus* her baton and boots. *And* she's going to teach me baton twirling. She would never even let me *touch* her baton before."

"She was always a pill," Marti muttered.

"Yeah, but she's changed," Faye said. "Ever since last night, when she told us she was going to get married, she's been almost human. So you guys want to come home with me after school and learn baton twirling? We'll have to do it in the garage, and be real quiet. My mother will probably still be crying. She'll have to get used to not calling my sister's husband 'that lowlife' once they're married. And my sister has to stay out of mother's face for a while. But do you want to come practice?"

"We've got rehearsals after school," Teena said. "And you've got to work on the posters for the play."

"Oh, yeah." Faye looked uneasy, but not guilty. "I just had a big scene with Mr. Razi. I told him I had to drop off the publicity crew."

"DROP OFF?" Teena and Marti cried at once.

"WHY?" Kerri demanded.

Faye looked uncomfortable, but she was not the kind of person who found other people, even the most popular girls in school, all that important. "I have to. My sister's moving out."

"So?" Marti challenged her. "You have to haul furniture or something?"

"So," Faye said, as if it should have been obvious, "I've got to get her to teach me baton twirling before she goes. Once she's married, she's not going to come over every day and teach me. This is my only chance."

"You are dropping off the publicity crew to learn

to throw a baton around?" Teena bit off each word, and left a pause after each.

Faye looked right back at her. "Listen, if I have a choice between learning baton twirling and making a bunch of posters . . ."

"You've got a conscience like a snake," Teena snapped.

Faye stalked away.

"That's really a neat way to get her to change her mind," Laurelle told Teena.

Marti looked worried. "Wasn't Faye the only one doing posters?"

Kerri nodded.

Marti looked even more solemn. "That means everybody has dropped off the publicity committee except Elliot Lofting. And he's doing the programs."

"Do you think he'll do posters, too?" Kerri asked.

Teena looked at her in disbelief. "Elliot Lofting on *posters*?"

"You don't have to be brilliant or anything to do posters," Kerri pointed out.

"Elliot Lofting," Teena said coldly, "wears brown polyester pants, with loafers. You have to at least have some dim idea of style if you're going to do posters."

Marti and Kerri and Teena went on agonizing over the poster problem the rest of the morning. In two classes, they got in trouble for whispering.

I don't think I've ever felt so out of everything. Even Preston and his kindergarten friends knew what they were going to do on Thanksgiving. Mike was having a birthday and getting his driver's license. Teena and Marti and Kerri were all wrapped up in the play. Even if Laurelle wasn't in it, at least she was working on makeup, so that she was *involved*. All the other people I knew, except Sherman, were looking forward to things that were important to them—things I had no part in. People in school looked at me with awe because I knew Mike Harbinger, but that had nothing to do with me. It wasn't like having friends who hung out with you because they thought you were neat.

There was always Sherman, of course, but Sherman was an eleven-year-old boy.

I saw him at a lunchroom table, saving me a seat as usual.

I sat down by myself at an empty table and opened my lunch, and he came over and sat beside me.

"Okay," he said. "Let's start over. What I'm going to do on Thanksgiving is have dinner with my family and their guests."

As usual, he had a fascinating lunch, mainly leftovers from one of his parents' weekend parties—stuffed mushrooms, tiny wedges of marinated eggplant, and some things I couldn't begin to identify.

"A lot of guests?" Now that I heard what I'd expected, it didn't seem that interesting.

"Everybody that my parents want to keep in good with." Sherman's father was running for mayor.

Marti and Teena and Kerri and Laurelle walked over to our table and sat down.

They glanced at Sherman, which was an improvement. At the beginning of the school year, they'd ignored him completely. But since he'd been seen with Mike and Mike's friends, Sherman had gotten a lot of prestige. He was still a wimp kid a grade ahead of his age in school, though, so nobody in junior high was really sure how to treat him now.

At any rate, Kerri and Marti and Teena were so intent on business they would barely have noticed anybody else at our table.

"So, listen." Teena, across from me, leaned over, like somebody proposing an international trade agreement. "We've decided you would be perfect for posters, Dez."

"I mean, you're the logical person." Marti, on my right, edged closer to me.

"You've got to," Kerri put in.

"I wouldn't know how to start," I said honestly.

"But we *want* you to," Marti said, as if that were a clinching point. "Besides, that way we'll all be in the play together."

I couldn't see how making posters would be the same as being in the play, but Teena and Marti and Kerri went on talking, each of them bringing up one argument after another.

"Look," Kerri said finally, "we can't put on a play with no posters."

"Besides," Marti put in, "Elliot Lofting absolutely refuses to do them. He says if he'd known he'd be stuck doing programs all by himself, he never would have let himself be suckered into the publicity committee."

"I'll talk to Mr. Razi," Teena said. "I know he can talk the art teacher into letting it be a special credit project. It will practically guarantee you an *A* in art."

A guaranteed *A* on my report card made those posters almost tempting. But there was more to it than that. While I hadn't even gone to tryouts for *The King and I,* if I did the posters, at least I'd have something to do with the play. When Marti and Kerri and Teena talked about it, I wouldn't feel left out. And this would be something *I* was doing, something more than just being "the girl who knows Mike Harbinger."

Only, I'd never made a poster before. "They might not look so great. . . ."

Marti and Kerri and Teena shrieked and punched my arm and all talked at once. After a reaction like that, I knew I couldn't back out.

After school, while I was getting my stuff from my locker, Teena and Marti and Kerri and Laurelle showed up with Elliot Lofting.

Even at twelve, Elliot Lofting is a depressing person. He's almost as tall as Teena, but thinner. His face is long and bony. His hair is dark brown, and straight, and he parts it on the side. His eyes are brown, as warm as a winter at the South Pole, and he looks as if he disapproves of life in general. In class, he tends not only to recite more than his share, but to talk on and on, as if it's his business to educate the people around him. You can see even the teachers starting to look bored when Elliot speaks.

Outside of class, Elliot talks as if he is doing it against his will and his better judgment.

"Okay," Marti told me. "Mr. Razi let us have the key to the room where you'll make the posters. Elliot will show you where all the poster stuff is, and where Faye left off."

The idea of spending any time with Elliot was about as appealing as trying to have a long spiritual conversation with Arnold Schwarzenegger. "What about Faye?" I asked. "She probably knows exactly . . ."

"You can't ask her," Kerri said flatly. "None of us is speaking to her."

Elliot walked through the halls a little ahead of me, I suppose to protect himself from the possibility that I might try to make friends with him.

I followed him down to the basement, past the furnace room and the custodian's supply room and the gym.

Elliot unlocked a door that read Storeroom.

The room was about twelve by sixteen feet, with a high, barred window. In the center of the gray vinyl floor were a long gray metal table, like the ones in the cafeteria, and two folding chairs. A stack of orange, yellow, and red poster board was propped at an angle against the window wall.

Elliot walked over to a gray metal cabinet on our left. When he opened the door, I saw on the shelves about a dozen jars of paint, along with brushes, paste, scissors, rulers, and pencils.

Right away, I had a feeling that this poster making was not a high-tech operation.

"They probably checked all this stuff out," Elliot said, "so you have to keep track of it."

"Where are the posters Faye did?" I wondered.

Elliot did help me search, I'll give him that. As I shuffled through all the poster boards against the wall, he steadied them.

We looked around the room, but there was no place a poster could have been hidden.

"There aren't any," he said finally.

"Elliot, I hadn't figured on that. I'm not sure how to start."

"Maybe when I get the programs figured out you can copy off them." He said it as if he knew he was making a wild and reckless promise that he would certainly regret.

"When will that be?" I pressed him.

"Well, I've got Math Club after school today. . . ."

"Tomorrow, could I see what you're doing? Where will you be making these programs?"

"They let me use one of the detention rooms near the office, but I can't have anybody hanging around in there. When I get something done, I'll let you know." Elliot handed me the keys. "Be sure to lock up when you leave. You'd be in big trouble if this stuff got ripped off." He walked out.

As I stood looking around the room, I began to think that I had let myself be talked into something I was going to regret.

The door opened, and Teena came in.

"I'm trying . . . I'm trying to figure out just how to go about this," I confessed.

Teena looked around the room. "Where are the ones Faye did?"

"She didn't."

Teena let out a long "Uhhh," a sound of pure disgust mixed with fury. "If I get my hands on that weasel!"

This was not the time to admit that I was not sure I wanted to do the posters. "Maybe she couldn't figure out how to start. I had thought I was just supposed to pick up from where she left off."

"I *told* her how to do them." Teena sat on the table, intense and businesslike. "What you want is a picture of something interesting, like Anna in a big hoop-skirt dress. And then you print all the information that will get people to come—like 'Teena Brannigan in *The King and I*'—and then the place and the date and the time."

"Just your name? What about Lars?"

"Well . . . okay. Teena Brannigan and Lars Svenson, then."

"And I have to put the name of the person who wrote *The King and I*."

Teena looked at me patiently. "Dez, haven't you ever seen a movie poster? Don't you read movie ads? They have, like, 'Sylvester Stallone' and then the name of the movie. His name is in bigger letters than anything, even the title of the movie. But they don't have who *wrote* it on the ad."

"You're not Sylvester Stallone, either, Teena."

"But the point is, the name of the star always comes first."

"I bet not always."

"Look, why would kids in this school read the posters? To find out who's in the play that they know."

"Believe me, Teena, everybody who knows you knows you're in the play."

"Hey, Dez." Sherman looked into the room. "Aren't you going to go get Aida?"

I was relieved to see him, since he probably saved me from a showdown with Teena. "Right!"

She got off the table. "I'll come down and see how you're doing, in case you need more advice or anything."

When I went up to return the keys, Mr. Razi was busy reading somebody out, so I just put them on his desk and hurried to go get my sister.

I walked with Sherman half a block before I asked casually, "Listen, you want to work on publicity with me, Sherman? Posters?"

"No," he said.

"I need you."

He just shook his head. Either he was sensitive that Teena and Marti and Kerri hadn't asked him, or he was still depressed about Thanksgiving.

I didn't mention the posters to my family or to Mrs. Farisee that evening. There's no sense talking about something you're supposed to do when you are seriously thinking of backing out of the project.

Two

At least Thanksgiving was not the only thing on my mind the next morning. I had to face the fact that I had no idea how to go about making posters to advertise a school play.

I didn't know who wrote *The King and I,* but I was pretty sure the author's name had to be included along with the dates and times of the performances. As for Teena, I had a feeling the rest of the players would have strong ideas about seeing only her name. And to list everybody in the cast would call for very, *very* small printing.

Maybe I could get some advice from Kerri or Marti at lunch, if I could get them away from Teena long enough. If they said everybody's name had to be listed, I could just say I was not that good at fine printing and resign then and there.

But Teena and Marti and Kerri had to take their lunches to the auditorium for a special rehearsal.

"Mr. Razi said the rate the cast is going, this play won't be ready by the time they leave for college," Laurelle told me as we walked down to the cafeteria. "When they do a musical like this for a junior high, they cut it down to an hour, and take out a lot of the talking. And those kids *still* have trouble remembering their lines. They should outlaw school plays."

"Laurelle," I confided, "I can't do the posters. I have no idea how to do posters for a play."

She slowed down. "You said you would."

"I can't."

She stopped cold. "Already none of us is speaking to Faye Brower. If you fink out after she did, I guarantee that nobody in the whole cast will speak to you for the rest of the year, and maybe not even in high school."

People in junior high had just *started* speaking to me. From the way they ignored Faye Brower, I could see how Teena and Kerri and Marti could make the rest of my school year miserable. As popular as they were, it was likely a lot of people would follow their lead. "Laurelle, would you help me?"

"Listen, I have never even used eyeliner! And I have to make up a bunch of junior high kids to look Siamese! I have to figure out how to make Lars Svenson look like a Siamese king!"

As we walked into the cafeteria, I looked around for Sherman. With Laurelle behind me, I hurried to the table where he sat. Without looking over his lunch, I opened my own. I waited a minute or two, so he wouldn't think I was putting pressure on him, and then said, "Sherman, you've got to help me. I don't even know how to *start* a poster."

"I've never made a poster in my life, Dez," he told me.

"Ask Elliot," Laurelle suggested.

I was beginning to feel that nobody in the world even wanted to understand my problem. "Laurelle, did you ever try asking Elliot Lofting for anything? Elliot Lofting strikes me as person who wouldn't give you a glass of water if your hair was on fire."

Laurelle opened her lunch. Sherman went on eating. So much for sympathy and concern, I thought.

After my last class, I got the keys to the storeroom from Mr. Razi, and went down there. From the gym came the thunk-thunk-thunk of basketballs and running feet. From the other end of the hall came the humming and *tahugga* of machinery. I opened the locker and looked at the paints and brushes. Then I sat on the floor and stared at the poster boards against the wall.

I heard the door of the room open and I turned, too downhearted to worry about Elliot Lofting seeing me sitting on the floor watching poster boards.

It was Sherman. "Aren't you going to go get Aida?"

"Yeah." I got to my feet. "I was just looking at this stuff."

He came over and squatted down and gazed at the poster boards. "There sure are a lot of them. A lot of Thanksgiving colors, too . . . orange, yellow . . ."

"Big deal," I muttered.

Sherman looked into the open cabinet. "Wow. Look at that paint and junk. Even brown paint."

"Thanks, Sherman. I feel all twittery at the thought of doing something with brown paint on yellow poster board." I shut the cabinet. "Let's go get Aida."

He didn't speak for most of the four blocks to her school. Then, suddenly, he said, "I guess I can."

"What?"

"I'll make some posters."

I was so relieved I almost hugged him.

I had no idea, of course, of the plot he was hatching.

That night at dinner Mrs. Farisee said, "I thought I might not go to my niece's for Thanksgiving."

My father glanced up, surprised. Mrs. Farisee had been with us less than a year, so we had no traditions built up, but I suppose he'd agreed, or just assumed, that she'd take holidays off.

"Her children," she explained. "They'd give a tag-team wrestler nervous indigestion."

It was not often Mrs. Farisee bothered to explain herself. I think she felt a little embarrassed, confessing less than a week before Thanksgiving that she had no plans for the holiday.

"So if you'd like me to stay around," she went on,

"I can make a proper dinner for you all. You should let me know right away so I can start planning."

While I sat mentally urging my father to accept Mrs. Farisee's offer, Antony and Aida watched him expectantly.

"That would be . . . fine." He still looked taken aback.

"Unless you've already made plans . . ." Mrs. Farisee said.

He hesitated a second, then he said, "Just to go to a restaurant. Eating at home would be much nicer. That is, if you don't mind two extra people. I've already asked them to join us for dinner. If it would be too much trouble . . ."

I waited, half afraid she'd say it would. Mrs. Farisee was a woman who spoke her mind, unless she was going for maximum effect, in which case her scowl carried more weight than an unabridged dictionary. Mrs. Farisee was not one to be mealy-mouthed about anything.

"That shouldn't be a problem," she said.

I didn't know whether she didn't want to be a grump, or whether she had no place else to go. Maybe her niece hadn't even invited her yet, and she was faced with killing the whole day, all alone.

Or maybe, just maybe, it was even more than being caught up in the holiday spirit. What if she really wanted to spend the holiday with us? Could it be that she'd gotten fond of us, that she'd started to think of us as her family?

The thought was almost scary. If Mrs. Farisee ever went soft, what could you count on in this world?

Meanwhile, I was eager to know who our guests would be. For a second, I thought maybe our mother had let our father know she wanted to come home to us, and he was saving it for a surprise. But I knew that if that happened he would never be mean enough to keep the news from us for a minute.

Then I thought maybe he'd invited Pat Troup. She and my father had gone out together a couple of times.

While having Pat come to dinner would be nowhere near as stupendous as having our mother return, Pat would be a neat guest. She was still in her early twenties, but she wasn't all hung up on clothes and makeup—she dressed as if she grabbed whatever she found lying on the floor of her closet. I liked the way she looked, as if she had more important matters on her mind. She did have important things on her mind, too. She was a newspaper reporter, and a very good one.

Two people, my father had said. Of course, Pat wouldn't leave her father alone on Thanksgiving. But my father would have to be so goofy in love with Pat *all* of us would know it before he'd invite Eleazar Troup to dinner. Mr. Troup disapproved of children, loathed our dogs, and had never spoken a civil word to my father.

Mr. Troup would have been the last person to think of himself as an ally of ours, but in a way he was.

24

Sherman's parents had never been happy about renting to a family with three kids and three dogs. They'd let us stay, but grudgingly. Then Harley Grove, Sherman's father, went in with his brother Bramwell on a deal to get the houses on our block condemned, tear them down, and put up condominiums. Since the houses were small and old and shabby, and since most of the people were renting from Sherman's parents, the Groves didn't get much resistance. Eleazar Troup was the only person I knew of who held out, refusing to sell. I had to respect him for that—and to be grateful to him, in spite of the fact that he'd never given me more than a glower or a growl.

Still, he wouldn't have been my choice for a holiday guest.

If my father hadn't invited Pat, who had he asked? Then I thought, Oh, no. What if he's gone back to dating some flashy girl?

I had to ask. "Who?"

"A friend," he said. "I used to know her before . . . I knew her a long time ago."

"Who's the other person?" my brother Antony asked.

"Her mother," my father told him.

"Oh, wow," I said, before I could stop myself. That meant this friend had been a mere *child* when he knew her—so she was probably heavily into lip gloss and string bikinis by now.

After the twins were in bed and Mrs. Farisee had

gone to her room, I went into the dining room. My father sat at the table, writing in a notebook. Whenever I felt sorry for myself having to share a bedroom with my brother and sister, I thought of our father sleeping on a Hide-A-Bed in the parlor, doing the work he brought home in the dining room.

I sat across the table watching him.

He closed the notebook. "What, Dez?"

"Who is she?"

"Who?"

"The woman who's coming to dinner. What's she like?"

"You'll meet her on Thanksgiving."

"Come on. Don't do that. I want to know what to expect."

"Her name is Irene Vardis and she's about my age."

I would have been relieved that he was interested in somebody his own age, except that I couldn't see how he could do better than Pat Troup. "How long have you known her?"

"You want her resumé?"

"When you invite somebody home to a holiday dinner, it's either some lonely person you feel sorry for, or it's somebody special."

"She's not lonely," he said.

"So have you actually been dating this person?"

"I ran into Irene when I went to the state mental-health convention earlier this month," he said. "We spent some time together there, and yes, I've been seeing her since."

"She's a psychologist, too?"

"She markets computer programs for doctors."

Even though I knew it would be a mistake, I had to ask. "Did you tell Pat?"

"I think you've had enough of a rundown on my private life." His tone was even, but I knew I had better not ask any more personal questions. I hoped that Pat would have her father over to her apartment Thanksgiving Day, instead of coming to his house. It would be terrible if she arrived next door just in time to see some other women sweep into our house.

I was uncomfortable, thinking I'd annoyed my father, so I was glad to change the subject. "Sherman and I are going to make posters for the school play, *The King and I.*"

"That's great." He was plainly pleased to have me getting more involved in school events.

"I don't know. I'm kind of nervous about it. I don't even know who wrote *The King and I.*"

"Richard Rodgers and Oscar Hammerstein the Second, from the book *Anna and the King of Siam.*"

"Do we have to put all that on the posters?" I asked.

"I think Rodgers and Hammerstein are entitled to a mention."

The minute we got to school the next morning, Sherman said, "Let's get the keys to the poster room from Mr. Razi. I could work for a few minutes before class."

He settled into that storeroom as if he had been born to make posters. He picked out three yellow and three orange poster boards and put them on the table.

I watched him carrying paint and brushes to the table. "What do you want me to do?"

I don't think he even heard me. He set a ruler and pencil on one of the orange boards and drew some lines on it, and by then it was time to go to class.

At lunchtime, he was waiting outside the cafeteria. "Let's go down to the storeroom," he greeted me. "Mr. Razi let me keep the keys."

Sherman was the kind of kid any teacher would trust with keys. He was the type who gets stuck with jobs like cleaning erasers, and puts his heart into it. He was somebody a teacher would assign to help some delinquent who can't figure out math, knowing the chore would be taken as a sacred obligation. Besides, Sherman's mother was on the school board and his father was running for mayor.

We took our lunches down to the storeroom. Sherman ate just part of the strange stuff he'd brought and then wiped his hands on his jeans and started drawing more lines on another poster board.

I licked off my fingers and stood watching him. "Do we start with a picture, or what?"

He didn't look up. "What you can do is go up to the library and see if you can find any pictures of

Siamese temples and people and stuff. Meanwhile, I'll work on the lettering."

After school, Sherman was waiting outside my last class. "I'll be down in the storeroom."

It was the first time he had been at school and not come with me for my sister.

It felt odd and a little uncomfortable to have him change the routine. At the same time, I was grateful that he was getting so involved.

"So I'll bring Aida back here," I said.

"It'd be better if you take her on upstairs to the library and see if you can check out more books with pictures of Siamese stuff before it's closed."

"Sherman, all I could find is in the reference section, and you can't check those out. Besides, I don't think you can bring a kindergarten kid into the junior high library."

"Okay. Why don't you guys go on to the public library, then. I'll stick around here and keep working."

"Won't you need the pictures?"

"Not for a while." He seemed almost eager to get rid of me.

I left. I was puzzled, and a little hurt that Sherman wanted to work alone. At the same time, I was relieved. I'd never imagined that I could do anything as easy as looking through books for my part of this undertaking.

Aida and I spent over an hour at the library, and

I checked out four books that had Siamese pictures in them. Going home, I thought how lucky I was that Sherman was taking so much responsibility for the project.

Looking back, I suppose I should feel stupid. But who in the world would have had the slightest suspicion that Sherman Grove, old wimpy, law-abiding Sherman, would do anything but what he was supposed to be doing?

Three

When Sherman came by for Antony and me in the morning, I tried to show him the books I'd got out of the library. He barely glanced at them. I couldn't help being annoyed, but there was no sense fussing at him—not if I was going to make him carry half of them.

Walking to school, I wondered what was going on between my father and Pat Troup, and how serious my father was about this Irene, and what she and her mother would be like.

Sherman, too, seemed to have a lot on his mind.

It was so early we didn't run into any other kids we knew. As Sherman and I walked into the junior high building, he said, "I'll go on down to the storeroom."

"Let me go to my locker first," I said.

"That's okay. You don't need to come down."

Ever since I'd moved to this town Sherman had

stuck to me like an unwanted nickname. Now, for two days he had been almost trying to get rid of me when he was working on the posters. And there had been his flare-up when I asked him about Thanksgiving.

I walked on alone. With time to kill, and Sherman to worry about, I cleaned out my locker. I was dusting off the shelf with a Kleenex when Teena and Kerri and Marti and Laurelle showed up.

"How are the posters coming?" Teena greeted me.

What could I say? Could I admit I had not touched a brush or drawn a line? Could I admit I had practically turned the whole job over to Sherman, when they didn't even know he was working on it?

I shrugged.

You don't shrug at the lead in a play who asks about the play's publicity.

"Listen," she said, "those things have to be done in time for people to see them and plan to come! They have to be up by this weekend."

"Oh, come on," Laurelle told her. "Everybody in school knows about the play. The only people that are going to come will be kids from school and their parents, if they can drag them."

Teena glared at her. "Just don't go out for cheerleading in high school, okay? I can hear you before a game—'It doesn't really matter who wins, guys, so don't knock yourselves out or anything.'"

After Teena stalked off, Laurelle asked me, "How far are you, really?"

"I got all the research done, and Sherman's actually working on the posters now."

"Research?"

"Pictures of Siamese people and temples and things. Listen, I have to go."

I realized I'd better see for myself how Sherman was doing. If those posters were a mess, I was in for a long, miserable school year.

When I got to the door of the storeroom, I found it locked.

I knocked.

There was no answer.

I rapped harder.

No answer.

"Sherman?" I called.

Then, "Sherman? Are you in there?"

I sat down on the floor and looked over my homework. When he showed up, I'd have to tell him the cast was getting anxious.

I waited until the bell rang, and then hurried to class.

At lunchtime, Sherman was not in the cafeteria.

I told myself I should be grateful that he was so wrapped up in the project. But I was even more sure that I should see for myself just what he'd done.

I hurried on down to the basement.

From the end of the hall, I saw him unlocking the door of the storeroom.

"Sherman!" I yelled.

He didn't even turn.

"Sherman!" I hurried toward him. "You'd just better wait!"

He stood, his hand on the knob.

When I reached him, he didn't look at me.

"Sherman, what is going on? Where were you this morning?"

"Working on posters."

That hurt. I never, never would have believed that Sherman could lie to me. "You were not. I knocked, and I waited right here until the bell rang."

"I was busy."

"You're trying to tell me you were in there and you didn't let me in?"

"I couldn't."

He had a closed, stubborn look. I told myself that blowing up at Sherman was not the way to find out what was going on. I tried to sound calm but firm. "How far are you on the posters, Sherman?"

"I'll get them done."

"Sherman, that's not what I asked. The play is next weekend."

"I know." But he didn't look at me.

I didn't feel hurt or angry anymore. I just felt absolutely sure there was something very, very strange going on. "Okay, Sherman. I got stuck with this job in the first place, and if those ads are not up by this weekend, I'm the one Teena and the rest are going to ostrich eyes."

He looked at me then. *"Ostrich eyes?"*

34

"Worse than Faye Brower. And nobody will even speak to her."

"You mean *ostracize*," he said.

One thing about having a wimp for a friend, you don't have to be embarrassed around him. "No kidding? I always wondered why people said that somebody who was shut out and ignored was being ostrich eyesed. But it makes sense. Ostriches do have a strange way of looking people. . . ." Then I remembered I was there to talk business. "Okay. So let's get to work, then."

"I don't need help."

"Sherman, I am not some kindergarten kid. I can paint well enough to fill in the lines."

"I don't want any help."

Nobody can be patient and reasonable forever. *"I'm not supposed to be helping you! You're supposed to be helping me!* And you're acting like James Bond or somebody! There must be materials for at least a dozen posters in there. That means we're supposed to get a dozen done by . . ."

"I'll finish them. I have to have them up this weekend."

There was something about the way he said it that cooled me right down. He didn't say it like someone who had to meet somebody else's deadline. He said it with the calm but solemn tone of somebody who is doing something very important . . . something all his own.

"I don't know what's going on in there, but I'm going to see." I tried to move him aside.

He shook his head, gripping the doorknob.

"Okay, Sherman. I'll just go get the whole cast down here and see if you can keep us all out."

For a minute, I was afraid he was going to make me do it. Then he opened the door and let me shove past him into the storeroom.

I had to reach around for the light.

When I found the switch and turned it on, I saw that he had stuck a piece of poster board between the bars and the glass so that nobody could look in the window.

And then I saw what he had been doing, shut up in that room.

"Oh, Sherman."

As strange as he'd been acting, I had never suspected this.

There was that long table, covered with eight posters of turkeys—brown turkeys, white turkeys, brown and white turkeys with red wattles. They weren't great, but you could tell they were turkeys. And under each, in big, wobbly letters, Sherman had painted a message:

THANKSGIVING'S NO TREAT
FOR THE BIRD THAT YOU EAT

and

DON'T MAKE THANKSGIVING A FOWL HOLIDAY—
SPARE A TURKEY'S LIFE

and

GIVE A TURKEY REASON TO BE THANKFUL—
HAVE A VEGETARIAN HOLIDAY DINNER

There were more. While Sherman was not much of an artist, he was good at making up messages.

The door opened, and Laurelle looked in. "Hi."

In spite of everything, you can't stop caring about a friend.

I stepped toward the door quickly, and switched off the light.

As I moved Laurelle back into the hall, Sherman followed.

"We'd better get to class." I shut the storeroom door.

Laurelle followed Sherman and me down the hall. "What I need is pictures of Siamese people. I'm still trying to figure out how to make Lars look Siamese."

"Right. Good idea." I hurried on.

"So could I see the pictures you have?" she asked.

"Sure," I told her.

There was a crush of kids going up and down the stairs. Sherman managed to edge his way through and escape.

"When?" Laurelle called after me, but I didn't answer.

At the end of the day, I rushed out of my last class and caught Sherman just as he was coming out of his.

"I'm not letting you out of my sight!" I grabbed his sweater.

"You have to pick up Aida."

"Not today. Mrs. Farisee is taking her right from school for a dental checkup."

Now that I had him, I wasn't sure what to do with him. I mean, a kid who is supposed to be making play posters and locks himself up to do turkey posters is not somebody you have to deal with every day. I remembered how hostile he'd been earlier about the whole subject of Thanksgiving.

If he was cracking up, it was my job, as his friend, to do something about it.

But what?

The first thing to do was get him where nobody could overhear.

I steered him down the stairs to the basement, heading for the storeroom.

He didn't say a word. He didn't try to explain.

"Sherman, you know you're going to be in serious trouble, don't you? That's school property you ripped off."

"I didn't rip it off," he said. "I just commandeered it. I'll replace it as soon as I get my allowance."

"One week's allowance wouldn't begin to . . ."

"Okay, I'll get an advance."

I could see I was not getting through to him. "Sherman, we're talking about time, too. You can't put back all the time I thought you were making posters for *The King and I*. I trusted you. Did you do one play poster? Even one?"

"Could we go into the storeroom so everybody won't be listening?" he asked.

There was nobody in sight but Laurelle, who was walking toward us.

At the door to the storeroom, Sherman said, "Let's just go in and tell her we're busy. Got the keys?"

"You had them," I said.

"I don't. I thought you did."

"You left them in the lock." Reaching past me, Laurelle turned the knob and pushed open the door.

It was light in the room. The poster board was gone from the window.

Sherman's work was still spread out on the long table. "I came in between classes to look for some Siamese pictures," Laurelle said.

"I did those," Sherman told her. "Dez didn't even know what was going on."

That's the thing about Sherman. He's always ready to take the blame when the two of us get in trouble. Only this time, the trouble was all of his making.

"Dez was *supposed* to know!" Laurelle snapped. "She *picked* you!"

Sherman didn't back down. "I'm very good at secret stuff. *You* wouldn't have known, if you hadn't gotten in."

"Where are the play posters?" Laurelle glared down at the table.

"I'll get them done," Sherman told her.

"*When?*" Laurelle seemed to be almost as bewildered as she was indignant.

"Right away," Sherman said. "I promise. I had to do the Thanksgiving posters first. By Monday, people start buying turkeys."

"But these things you made are telling them not to," Laurelle pointed out.

Sherman nodded. "That's why they have to be up by this weekend."

"So this is what we've got. The play is in eight days, and you've done eight *turkey* posters and not one for *The King and I*. Why, Sherman, *why?*"

He looked down at his work. "When I was about . . . I guess four or five . . . my folks took me out to a turkey farm. They had told me I could pick my own turkey."

His voice was so low it was hard to hear him. "One turkey came right to me. 'That one,' I said. I could just tell this was my turkey. And I thought how it would be to ride home snuggled against those white feathers."

Sherman kept looking down at the table. "The man showing us around said, 'That one,' to a boy, and then took us down a dirt path to a shed with one of those wavy tin roofs. My father gave him money, and I stood and waited to take my turkey home."

Sherman was quiet for a second, then he said, "After a while, the boy came in the shed carrying it.

It had no head and no feet—and they'd pulled all its feathers off. But I knew this was my turkey. This was the one I'd picked. My father had to put it down and run after me.

"On Thanksgiving Day, they brought it to the table, roasted. And my father had to run after me again."

I realized now why he'd been so touchy when I asked him about Thanksgiving.

"Turkeys were smart birds once," Sherman said. "They were beautiful and agile, and they could fly. Then we started raising them for food. We bred them stupid, because all we wanted was meat and no trouble. Since white meat is more popular, we bred them with such huge chests they can't fly, and their poor legs can barely support their bodies. Nowadays most aren't even on farms. They're raised in cages, packed so tight they can't even lift their wings. Their beaks are seared off with a hot iron so they won't jab one another."

It was probably the first time Laurelle Carson had given Sherman Grove her complete attention.

"After you see animals alive," Sherman said, almost to himself, "the only way you can eat them is if you don't think about what you're doing. Veal calves are kept in crates so small they can't turn around. They never get to walk, until the day they're killed—when they're about four months old. Mother pigs live chained to the floor. They get so crazy, they just stand and swing their heads all day, day after day. But they turn out a lot of baby pigs for people to eat. You see all this stuff about how much fun fishing is, and you never really look at the fish flopping around, suffocating to death."

"You don't eat meat at all?" Laurelle asked.

"Not meat or fish or fowl," Sherman said.

"What do your folks say about it?" she pressed.

"First they sent me to a shrink, and then they let me stop going for a while. Now that I've quit wearing leather, they've decided to send me again. They're still looking for a psychiatrist who agrees that not wearing leather is a sign of emotional illness."

"That's dumb," Laurelle said. "There are plenty of neat shoes that aren't leather."

"I think my mother takes it as a personal attack," Sherman confided.

"Of course." I could understand why. "She must have a dozen fur coats and jackets."

"You know what students in England do when they see somebody on the street wearing a fur coat?" Sherman was so deep into the subject he'd forgotten how much trouble he was in with Laurelle and me. "They follow the person around, muttering, 'Gross. Gross. Gross.'"

"You can't follow your own mother around, muttering 'Gross,' " I warned him. "Especially not in public."

"I doubt if it's even legal," Laurelle observed. "I think it's harassment or something."

"Probably," Sherman admitted. "Animals caught in leghold traps try to chew their own legs off. Trappers can leave animals caught like that for days before they come bash their heads in and skin them. But you can't insult somebody who wears the skins."

"I'll tell you something, Sherman," I warned. "If you start following your mother around mumbling 'Gross,' you may end up with a shrink who's on her side."

I think Laurelle realized she'd let herself be sidetracked from her hard-hitting prosecutor role. "Meanwhile," she told Sherman, "you've been here making anti-turkey-eating posters instead of what everybody thought you were doing." She looked at Sherman narrowly. "If your mother can afford all those fur coats, how come you can't buy your own poster board and paints?"

"Can you see me making these posters at *home*?" Sherman asked her. "My folks would put in an emergency call to any shrink who'd listen. Anyway, I already told Dez I'll put back everything I used."

"Boy, you'd better," Laurelle told him. "You steal school property, that's probably a state offense."

"I didn't steal it," Sherman said hotly. "It wasn't the stuff that mattered, it was the *cover*. I mean, what's a better place to make posters than a place where you're supposed to be making posters?"

"You made them all right." Laurelle's voice had gotten louder. "You used all but four boards, and *we don't have one poster for the play.*"

"The four left are for play posters," Sherman said mildly. "I figured they wouldn't let me put the turkey ones up in school."

Laurelle's voice was getting higher. "When they gave you twelve pieces of board that meant they expected twelve posters!"

"I know. I'll do them," Sherman insisted.

Laurelle's voice sank to a low rasp. *"On what?"*

"On the backs of the turkey ones. I'll put them around town with the turkey side out until Wednesday, and then turn the play side out."

"That is the dumbest idea I ever heard," Laurelle declared flatly.

I wasn't absolutely sure she was wrong, but Sherman was my good, true friend. "I don't know," I said. "It's economical."

Laurelle looked at me helplessly. "How are you going to get twelve posters done? They'll have to be up at least a few days before the play."

"I'll get here first thing tomorrow," I promised, "and work every lunch hour and after school."

We had pork roast for dinner that night. I looked at it, and I thought about the chained pigs and the piglets.

"None for me, please," I said.

Mrs. Farisee looked offended. "I always cook pork well done."

"I know. I just don't think I can eat any," I told her.

"Do you feel all right?" my father asked.

"Yes," I said. "But, please, no pork."

He glanced at Mrs. Farisee, who shook her head but put no pork on my plate.

Four

The next morning, Sherman was at the door before I'd even finished breakfast.

"You may not come here at the crack of dawn and disrupt our whole morning," Mrs. Farisee greeted him.

"We have to get to school early to do posters for the school play," I told her. "It's only for a few more days."

She was still grumping when Sherman and I left the house, hustling Antony along between us.

Because it was so early, we made sure Antony could get into his school, and then we hurried on to the junior high.

Laurelle was waiting outside the storeroom.

"So how are we going to do this?" she asked.

I was amazed.

Sherman recovered first. He let us in and said,

"How about Dez and I do the pictures, and you do the lettering? Unless you'd rather do the pictures."

"Nah. I'll do anything." She pulled a chair up to the table.

At noon, the three of us went back down to the storeroom.

While Sherman opened paint jars, Laurelle unwrapped a chopped olive sandwich.

"We had leg of lamb last night," she said. "All I could think of was those petting zoos your parents take you to, and the Easter and Christmas exhibits in the mall, with the lambs . . ."

I nodded, thinking of the live baby chicks I'd seen in store windows around Easter.

By the time the bell rang, we had a total of six play posters finished.

After school, I picked up Aida and brought her back to the storeroom. We even put her to work coloring large things like skirts.

We finished two more posters, so that we had used the backs of all the turkey posters.

"The ones to put up in school we can do Monday," Sherman said.

"So how are we going to post these eight, and where?" I asked. "We have to put them where we're allowed to, or they'll just get ripped down."

"How about in shop windows, on the inside?" Laurelle suggested.

Sherman looked dubious. "Do you think many

businesses would let us put Don't Eat Turkey signs in their windows?"

"Anybody will let us put up a poster for *The King and I*," she said. "If you're in business in this town, you can't refuse to let the junior high school stick a plug for their play in your window."

"They're not going to ask why the back of it says Don't Eat Turkeys?" Sherman asked.

"We're just going to have to find business people who don't mind," I said firmly. "And if we can't find eight, we'll have to put the rest of the posters wherever we can, with the turkey side out, and then turn them late Wednesday."

"When do we do it?" Laurelle asked.

"How about tomorrow morning?" I suggested.

"Okay." Laurelle was brisk. "So who's going to take the posters home tonight?"

Sherman waited for somebody to volunteer, but nobody did. Finally he said, "I guess I'll have to, and hope I don't get caught."

We agreed to meet on the corner by his house at eight the next morning.

I don't know. Was it that Sherman just happened to find the only two people in the school who would go along with him? Maybe. Before Mike and his friends took up with us, Sherman and I were outcasts. But Laurelle was part of the most popular group in school, and people like that are usually careful not to do anything that might hurt their prestige.

Somehow, Sherman had got us to see something we'd never thought about before.

When three people see in a different way than they always have, that might be enough to make them feel together. And when they decide to *do* something about it, then they're a group.

Or a conspiracy.

Aida and I helped Sherman carry the posters home. Even with *The King and I* sides out, I was a little bit nervous about it, especially since his family didn't cherish mine.

Sherman's driveway was shaped like a horseshoe, curving off the street, easing past his house, curving back to the street. Straightened out, it would have been nearly half a block long.

At the moment it was full of cars—regular cars, press cars, TV vans—and people, a couple with cameras on their shoulders.

I wondered who in the house was sick or hurt or being arrested. If I hadn't been holding posters I would have reached for Sherman's hand.

Then I heard his father's voice, hearty and sincere. It was not the voice of a man in trouble. It was the voice of a man running for office.

I should have realized that Sherman was *used* to press cars and reporters and photographers in his driveway. Pat Troup, I saw, was not one of the reporters.

By now, I was interested. Holding Aida's hand, I edged with Sherman around the back of the crowd until I could see through to the center of all the action.

Mr. Grove, in a three-piece business suit, and Mrs. Grove, in a lilac-colored dress, were standing at the foot of the steps leading to their front porch. Behind them, looking as if she wanted to back up the steps into the house, stood the Groves' latest maid.

Closer to the cameras was a heavyset man with gray hair and beard, wearing a jacket with fringed sleeves, jeans, and boots. "Who is he?" I whispered.

"Colonel Fairbrook," Sherman muttered. "He owns more of this town than my family does. He has a big ranch. . . ."

"Here we go!" Colonel Fairbrook boomed, and two men lifted a wire cage out of the back of a station wagon parked in front of the house.

Keeping his face turned toward the cameras, the colonel said, "As you fine people know, I have for years maintained that our state bird should be . . ."

"Ducks!" Aida whispered.

She was right. In the cage were two white ducks.

". . . the duck," continued the colonel. "The duck—at home on land, on water, in the air. And this is a state full of prime land, of lakes, of open skies. I would never presume to replace that traditional American Thanksgiving bird, the turkey, but I must point out that the duck is not only smarter, but a heck of a lot prettier!"

Even the reporters laughed. The men set the cage down in front of the Groves.

"The colonel raises ducks," Sherman muttered, "as a business."

I squatted beside him. "You mean for . . ."

Sherman sat down. "Like chickens, turkeys . . ." Then he rested his forehead against his knees.

"And so, in the spirit of the great American holiday, it is my pleasure to present to the next mayor of this town—and his lovely lady—America's *other* noble bird." The colonel offered his hand to Harley Grove, who had to lean over the cage to take it, while the photographers got more pictures.

"So what are you going to do with your ducks?" a reporter asked Sherman's father.

"You going to keep them for pets?" another reporter asked.

Harley Grove smiled into the cameras. "We all know it's against the city ordinance to keep anything like ducks or chickens in this neighborhood. It would certainly . . . ah . . . ruffle a few feathers . . .if your next mayor laid an egg by ducking a law."

Sherman shook his head, not even lifting it from his knees.

"No, no," Fairbrook said loudly. "These fine fowl will be visiting in the Groves' backyard for only a final few days."

I have never felt quite so sick and furious and generally betrayed by the whole dumb world.

"So you're having these ducks for Thanksgiving?" a reporter asked Mrs. Grove.

"Of course not!" she said with a smile. "Our family has always had a traditional American Thanksgiving dinner . . . turkey with all the trimmings."

"So what will you do with the ducks?" another reporter asked.

Mr. Grove spoke up heartily. "Well, first, after Thanksgiving we'll freeze the turkey leftovers, instead of disguising them day after day for the next week."

The people around him chuckled.

"We'll give that turkey dinner a few days to fade into memories," Harley Grove went on, "and then we'll have . . ."

". . . the most succulent, satisfying, and *state*-worthy birds any American family can be proud to enjoy. A genuine duck dinner!" Fairbrook put his arm around Harley Grove's shoulders and grinned into the cameras.

"I assume you're invited to this feast," a reporter told the colonel.

"Of course. Colonel Fairbrook will be our guest of honor." Mrs. Grove stepped closer to her husband as the photographers took more pictures. I couldn't help noticing that she arranged it so that her husband would be in the center of all the pictures.

Sherman stood up. Hugging his posters close, he edged around the crowd to the back of the house.

I figured it would be a while before Sherman's parents came in. Besides, this was no time to leave him.

Aida and I followed him up to his room. He shoved

the posters he'd carried under his bed. I set the others on the rug beside him, and he shoved them under the bed, too.

I didn't know what to say to him. "I'm sorry" was too feeble. I sat on the floor, Aida beside me.

She looked at Sherman, and her voice was almost a whisper. "That man gave your folks those ducks for a present, and they're going to *eat* them?"

"Shh." I put my arm around her.

"You'd better get Aida home, Dez." Sherman didn't look up. "Mrs. Farisee is going to have a fit if you're late."

"I could call her."

"I'd just as soon be alone, thanks."

I could imagine how he felt, laboring for days over posters asking people not to eat a turkey for Thanksgiving, only to find two ducks in his own backyard waiting to be slaughtered.

On the way home, my sister asked suddenly, "They're really going to kill those ducks?"

"Well . . . maybe something will come up." How could I come right out and admit the ducks were doomed?

And then another thought struck her. "They said they're going to eat turkey for Thanksgiving. Does that mean they kill a turkey to eat for Thanksgiving?"

"They probably buy one that's already dead."

"What did it die of?"

I couldn't out and out lie to her. "Turkeys are raised

to be killed, mainly for Thanksgiving and Christmas dinners."

She stopped and looked at me in shock. "*Why?*"

"Because people like the taste of them." Maybe I should have lied to her, I thought.

"That's the dumbest reason I ever heard!" she blurted.

She walked the rest of the way home with her head down.

Once we got in the house, though, she had so much to do she forgot about ducks and turkeys. She had to change her clothes, and go out back to wrestle Antony and the dogs, and try to smuggle the dogs in past Mrs. Farisee to watch television.

There are some good things about being five.

We had meat loaf for dinner. Once you start thinking about what you're eating, you realize just what meat loaf is. Ground beef, I thought. Ground beef is a ground-up cow.

"No meat, please," I said.

"This is getting ridiculous," Mrs. Farisee exploded. "Is this some kind of fad, or some quack reducing diet?"

"I'll talk to Dez about it tomorrow." My father had just stepped into the kitchen. "Why can't we keep a drinking glass in the bathroom?" He was going out to dinner, which may have made Mrs. Farisee a little touchy about two people skipping her meat loaf.

We couldn't keep glasses in the bathroom because

the twins were always borrowing them to keep marbles or broken crayons in. "I still think we should get one of those paper cup dispensers," I said, relieved to get the subject off what I wasn't eating.

"And you know what would happen," Mrs. Farisee said. "The twins would pull out cups to float in the bathtub, or rinse watercolor brushes in, and I would be picking up paper cups and wiping up whatever leaked out when the cups soaked through."

After we finished the dishes, I went to my room to do some homework. When I got out my binder, I came across the pamphlets and magazines Sherman had given me, put out by People for the Ethical Treatment of Animals.

I think it was the pictures that got to me most—cows in a feedlot, mired up to their bellies in mud and worse; pigs forced to crawl on broken legs out of a truck to the slaughterhouse; live chickens packed so tight their feet had grown over the wire on the bottoms of their cages.

As soon as I heard my father come out of the bathroom, I met him in the hallway.

His hair was still damp, and he was fresh-shaven, wearing his best suit and a brand-new shirt. The real jolt was that he wasn't wearing his glasses.

After my mother had left us, he'd gone through a phase where he wore contact lenses and gold chains, got his hair styled like Steve Winwood's, and dated women who hadn't even outgrown Stri-Dex medicated pads. It passed. Even before he dated Pat Troup he'd gone back to wearing his glasses and dressing like a parent.

Now he was back to contacts.

Naturally, I pretended not to notice. You don't want to embarrass your father by asking, "Hey, where are your glasses?"

But I wondered if it was safe for him to drive after not wearing his contacts for months.

"Are you going to be on the freeway?" I asked.

"No, I'm going to be at a concert."

"I'm just worried about your driving without your glasses."

"Dez, I can see better with contacts."

I could hardly ask him to take an eye test before I let him go out. "I need to talk to you."

"Not about my eyesight."

"No. About me."

We went into the parlor and sat on the sofa. It's not easy trying to talk seriously with somebody who's worried about the time, so I got right to the point.

"I think I'm going to be a vegetarian," I said.

He looked surprised. "Why?"

"Because meat is animals. And we make them suffer even before we kill them. I've been eating meat just because that's how I was brought up, and because everybody else does, and I never thought about it before."

He didn't seem upset—or else he didn't want to

get into an argument that would make him late for the concert. "How are you going to get enough protein?"

"I'll find out. I'll study it."

He nodded. "I respect your decision. As a matter of fact, I'm touched that you're willing to go to some trouble out of concern for other beings. If you can stay healthy, it's fine with me."

I realized how lucky I was to get so much support from my father, whatever the reason. "So will you tell Mrs. Farisee?"

"No, you will. If you can stand up to her on this, you'll know you're truly committed."

I guess you shouldn't expect to get everything you want when you negotiate with a parent. Especially one who's on his way somewhere.

Mrs. Farisee was still in the kitchen, leafing through *The Joy of Cooking*.

I sat down across the table from her. When she looked up, I almost lost my courage, but I remembered what my father had said. If I backed down before I even started, it didn't say much for my being committed.

"I'm not going to be eating meat anymore," I told her. "Or poultry. Or fish."

She looked at me for a long minute. "Why?"

"Because . . . I care about the animals."

Mrs. Farisee has this talent for keeping her face absolutely unreadable. "Did you tell your father?"

"Yes. It's fine with him."

"I hope you don't expect me to cook you any special meals."

"Oh, no," I assured her hastily.

"How are you going to get enough protein?"

"I will study that. And I'll be sure it won't put you out in any way."

"I suppose it's between you and your father. But I tell you this—if you come up with any more strange notions, don't expect me to go along quietly."

Five

I got up before anyone the next morning, and fixed myself some toast and juice.

My father came into the kitchen in his pajamas and robe, looking half-awake.

I put on the water for his coffee. "I have to get over to Sherman's."

"This early?"

"We have things to do." Before my father could wake up enough to ask more questions, I kissed him and backed out of the room.

It was a clammy, gray morning, and I trudged along pulling the twins' red wagon, my brother's navy blue knit cap pulled down over my ears, the collar of my jacket up, and the chill creeping through my jeans. I kept my head down, partly from cold, partly in hopes nobody would recognize me. At least it was early and chilly enough that few people would be out.

I pulled the wagon up the Groves' long, curved driveway and around the side of the house.

Then—I couldn't help myself. Leaving the wagon, I looked around for the ducks.

The cage was far behind the house, near the tall back hedge.

As I squatted there, the ducks looked at me over those long orange bills. There they were, crammed into a cage with only a casserole dish half full of water. They couldn't swim or even walk around, and they didn't have a fit, or hiss or cower when a human came to look at them. Animals seem to take misery better than people do.

I walked back to the wagon.

Under Sherman's window, I stopped and picked up a handful of gravel from the path.

I don't know how many movies I've seen where somebody throws gravel at the window to wake the person inside. I suppose that's why I just naturally did it.

"Hey!"

In the movies, they never check to be sure the window is closed.

I was scared that Sherman's parents had heard him yell. But you don't run out on your best friend. It was a temptation, though.

I was sitting in the wagon when Sherman came stomping around from the back of his house in jeans and old sneakers, with his jacket only half-buttoned.

"What are you doing throwing stones through my window?" he demanded, trying to keep his voice down. "You got my whole room full of rocks and dirt!"

"What are you doing with your stupid window open in November, and no screen in it?" I flared back.

"I had it open so I could hear you when you showed up, and I had the screen off so I could lean out and tell you I'd be right down, without waking my folks."

"Oh."

"So if you'll wait here, without throwing anything else into my room, I'll start bringing the posters down."

He had to make two trips, but I didn't offer to go upstairs and help him. If his parents woke up and found him and me with a bunch of Don't Eat Turkey posters, there was no telling how they'd react.

As Sherman put the second load of posters on top of the first, I said, "I guess you talked to your folks about the ducks."

He took the wagon handle. "They said: A, Colonel Fairbrook is an important supporter of my father's and they are certainly not going to offend him by not keeping his present; B, it's against the ordinance to keep ducks in our neighborhood; C, Colonel Fairbrook is already invited to eat those ducks at our house; D, I am not to bring up the subject again no matter what." He trudged toward the street, hauling the wagon.

Sherman's neighborhood was so fancy it had no sidewalks, just huge houses on enormous lots, with a lot of trees and hedges fit for a castle. The roads didn't even go straight, but curved so that even the corners were rounded.

Laurelle was waiting under a towering pine. She was wearing old jeans and sneakers, with a dark blue quilted jacket and gloves, and a knit cap like mine pulled down over her ears. Like me, she looked dressed for a mission, like somebody out of *The Guns of Navarone*.

Neither Sherman nor I mentioned the ducks again. Explaining to Laurelle would have just made us think about them more.

The three of us took turns pulling the wagon and steadying the cargo.

We would have had no trouble putting just *The King and I* posters in windows. We could have put them all in shops in that one mall. But people got strange and uneasy when they saw the turkey side, and made excuses not to take one.

We went to three malls, and didn't get a single poster into a store window.

Finally, we trudged on over to the Rancho Grande Mall, the shabbiest shopping center in town. Sherman's uncle Bramwell owned it.

"I don't know," I told Sherman. "I have a funny feeling about trying your uncle's mall without him knowing about it."

But Sherman had been getting steadily more tense and determined, so by now there was no use arguing with him.

The Rancho Grande Mall had a market, a deli, a locksmith, a few repair shops, a pizza parlor, and the Mona Lisa Salon de Beauté.

Sherman led us toward the Mona Lisa.

"Oh, come on, Sherman," I protested.

"You know them in there," he reminded me.

"One haircut. *One haircut* I got from them. That doesn't make us *buddies*."

"So it's easier to ask a stranger if you can put a turkey poster in her window?" he demanded.

"Yes," I said. "Yes."

But he walked right to the door.

"Is this is where you get your hair cut?" Laurelle looked in the Mona Lisa window. There were pictures of hairstyles from ten years ago, and the beauty supplies on display had faded labels.

"Once," I said. "When I washed my hair with leftover varnish my brother and sister had poured into a shampoo bottle. That's why I had to have it so short."

She looked as if I'd just told her Mel Gibson was afraid of cars. "You mean it was all by accident?"

Sherman lifted a double-sided poster off the wagon. "I'll even come in with you."

Lisa was sitting at the front desk, reading the *National Enquirer.* The third button down on her pink nylon uniform was missing, which was understandable—she was somewhat stocky and had large bosoms. She had tinted her hair more of a lemon shade since I'd last seen her, and her eye shadow was a frosted turquoise. As we walked in, she glanced up.

"What's this?" She looked wary, as if we'd come weeks late for trick or treats.

"We've got . . ."

"We've got a poster we wonder if we could put in your window." Sherman showed her the *King and I* side and then the turkey side.

Mona came out from behind a curtain at the back of the shop and stood with her arms crossed, staring at the turkey side. She was considerably thinner than Lisa but her hair was pouffed out even more.

Lisa put down the paper. "You want to stick that up in *our* window?"

Sherman nodded.

"Why are the two sides different?" Mona wanted to know.

Sherman looked at me helplessly.

"To save poster board," I explained.

"Uh huh." Mona's voice had gone even more flat.

Lisa fixed Sherman with a hard gaze. "Did you ask your uncle if you could put that up in his mall?"

Sherman was beginning to look anxious. "No, ma'am."

"What do you think he'd say?" Lisa persisted. She didn't even wait for Sherman to answer. "Bramwell Grove would say that was no kind of poster to have in his mall just before people were fixing to buy turkeys. If anybody had that poster displayed, it would irk him." She looked at Mona. "Wouldn't it irk him?"

"It would irk him like crazy." Mona took the poster out of Sherman's hands.

She put it in the middle of the facial scrub and moisturizer display, the turkey side facing out.

"Wow!" Sherman looked solemn, like a kid who had gotten some present he'd given up on ever having. "Wow!"

I thought we should ask her to turn the play side out by Thursday, so people would see it, but then I realized that would sound as if I didn't think many people came into the salon, so I kept quiet.

"That's amazing," Laurelle marveled when we left the Mona Lisa.

"His uncle has that effect on people," I confided.

"Why don't we go in the other shops and say you're Bramwell Grove's nephew, and you want to put a poster in their window?" Laurelle suggested.

Sherman looked uneasy. "That would be putting pressure on them."

"But it worked," Laurelle pointed out.

Mona stepped out of the Salon de Beauté and stood leaning against the doorjamb with her arms folded.

"That's because they can't stand my uncle," Sherman told Laurelle. "I can't go in all the shops and ask if they'll put up a poster to annoy my uncle."

"They wouldn't let you anyway," Mona volunteered. "They'd have him and the meat manager at the market on their necks. Phoebe at the shoe repair, she'd put one up, but nobody else would. Give me one for Phoebe."

Sherman handed her another turkey poster.

This was my chance. "Listen," I said to Mona, "would you see that the posters are turned around before Thursday so that people going by see the ad for the play, too?"

"Sure." I guess she figured Bramwell Grove would be irked enough by then. "You know where else you should try?" she suggested. "You should try the SPCA thrift shop."

Sherman looked excited. "I never thought of that!"

We thanked Mona, and she headed for the shoe repair shop with the placard, while we headed out of the mall.

It was a long walk to the thrift shop, and the women there weren't sure they should let us put up the poster, for fear of offending people who weren't vegetarians.

A skinny young woman in tattered old jeans and a faded flannel plaid shirt stopped rummaging through the bin of fifty-cent shoes in order to listen to the discussion. Her long brown hair was thin and scraggly, and her eyes had the kind of quiet, humble look of somebody who's gotten used to being hurt. Finally, she broke in. "How many of those do you need to put up?"

"We have six left," Sherman told her.

"I can stick one in my window. I rent a room over a Chinese take-out place, so there's a lot of foot traffic."

"Hey, that's great!" I told her.

"And my boyfriend's got a van," she added. "It's not classy, but if he put a poster in the window, it would be moving around so plenty of people would see it."

"Perfect!" Laurelle chimed in.

As Sherman picked up two turkey posters, the woman said, "I can get them to put one up in the Chinese place. They sure as heck won't be selling turkey dinners."

She even promised to see to it personally that all the posters were turned to show the play side by Thursday.

You miss a lot if you overlook down-and-out people.

It took us the rest of the afternoon to place the last three posters—one in an auto body repair shop, one in a cubbyhole about six feet wide that had a sign Sewing and Alterations, and the last in a store that sold plastic foam. Everybody agreed to turn the posters Wednesday, too.

As we were trudging home, I felt tired, satisfied that we'd got all the posters up, but thinking it was pretty ironic we'd spent the day trying to save turkeys when there were two ducks in Sherman's own backyard waiting to be slaughtered.

Laurelle seem preoccupied, too. Then she said, "I've been thinking."

Sherman and I stopped to hear what she'd been thinking. She wasn't just one of the most popular girls in school, now. She was a person who had worked hard with us when there was absolutely nothing in it for her except a clean conscience.

She sat on the wagon, looking as if she was uncomfortable saying what was on her mind. "The only thing is, what if some people see the posters and don't buy a turkey for Thanksgiving? What if they buy ham instead?"

Sherman sat on the wagon beside her. "I think anybody who understands enough not to buy a turkey would understand enough not to buy a ham. I hope so."

I could see that he was worried, though. "Look," I put in, "there's no way we can make Don't Eat Ham posters and get them up before Thanksgiving."

"Before Christmas, maybe," Laurelle murmured.

When this girl got committed, she got committed.

I could see Sherman getting interested. "We'd have to have a place to make the posters. We have no excuse to use the storeroom. We could buy the materials. Only, it took us all day just to get eight posters up, and we had the *King and I* sides going for us."

"What if we put leaflets in all the play programs?" Laurelle asked. "At least a couple of hundred people would be sure to see them. We could get to all those people before they even started planning Christmas dinner."

I was amazed. "Laurelle Carson, I think you may be some kind of a genius."

Sherman took only a second to digest the idea. "We'd need a picture of a pig. . . ."

68

The idea got hold of me, too. "Why not a cow, and a calf, and a lamb, and a chicken? Why not go for broke?"

"Sure! Why not?" I've never seen Sherman so excited. "And I can write about how they're all raised and killed."

"Do you think we can get permission from the school to put them in the programs?" I asked.

"I don't think we should even try," Laurelle said. "If the SPCA is nervous about Don't Eat Turkey posters, you can imagine how the school will be about Don't Eat Animals fliers. We'll be in less trouble doing it without permission than doing it after we're told not to."

"Boy, Laurelle." Sherman stared at her. "You could be a great lawyer some day, if you stay out of jail long enough."

"Either way, if we do the fliers, we're in trouble," she warned.

I nodded. "But now that we've thought about doing them, we can't chicken out. It's too perfect an idea."

"Wait a minute," Sherman said. "Say we make a couple of hundred fliers. How do we get them into the programs? Elliot Lofting is doing those."

But Laurelle was not even slowed down. "We'll have to help Elliot with them."

"Help Elliot Lofting?" Sherman echoed what I was thinking.

"He's the only person working on programs. Besides, I bet nobody in the world has ever volunteered to help Elliot Lofting before. We'll help with the programs, and we'll volunteer to hand them out. A bunch of kids have signed up to usher, but you and Dez are on the publicity committee, right? So posters and programs are the publicity committee's business. We can't risk any of the ushers spotting the fliers."

"We don't want to get anybody else in trouble, either," Sherman put in.

Sherman is probably the nicest conspirator anybody could hope to be in a plot with.

"We'll tell Elliot he should supervise the ushers." I could see the logic in the plan, now. "He'll like that— a whole bunch of kids for him to order around. Sherman and I will stand at the door and hand out the programs, and then the ushers can show people to their seats."

"I should help hand them out, too," Laurelle said. "But if I drop off the makeup committee, I don't think Razi would ever speak to me again."

"We'll have only the Saturday performance to do it." Sherman looked grim. "Once the teachers are on to those fliers, they'll make sure there aren't any in the programs on Sunday."

"They may have a strong suspicion how they got into the programs," Laurelle murmured. "Which means, when we show up for the Sunday matinee, they may be waiting for us."

The more complications she brought up, the scarier the whole thing seemed, but I couldn't back down now. "We'll just tell the truth. When a kid in my last school ran all the band's drumsticks through a pencil sharpener, he only got a week's detention. So, Sherman will write the fliers, and you and I can find pictures of animals. . . ."

"I'm loaded with animal pictures," Sherman said.

I didn't feel bad about him taking on most of the work. I'd seen how he could produce when he was inspired.

"We've got a lot to do," Laurelle said. "We have to finish the four play posters for school and get them up by Tuesday."

"We should be able to put the fliers together Tuesday afternoon," Sherman said, "and take them by a copy shop Wednesday at the latest."

I began calculating in my head. "So at a nickel a page, say three hundred pages . . ."

"I can kick in ten dollars." All in all, Laurelle was a good person to be in a plot with.

Sherman's house was on my way home.

The two of us walked along, Sherman pulling the wagon. At last he said, "How can I put up turkey posters and make program inserts and leave two ducks in my own yard waiting to be killed?"

"I've been thinking about them."

When we got to his house, we left the wagon in the side yard and walked around to the back. The ducks were standing in a corner of the cage, but they looked at us through the wire patiently and humbly. There was only a little muddy water left in the casserole dish.

Sherman squatted by the cage. "They can't fly, they can't swim, they can't move two feet in any direction. Some life, huh?"

"Even with two of us, we couldn't just walk off with them, Sherman. We couldn't go down the street each carrying a duck without being noticed."

"I know," he said.

"This is serious. This is not something your parents would take lightly."

"I know," Sherman repeated, but I could tell he was waiting for me to go on.

"I suppose you're thinking who I'm thinking," I said.

I could see he'd been waiting for that. "You figure he would?"

"Are your parents home?"

"They're out for the day."

We walked through the laundry room into the kitchen. Sherman punched in the number, and then handed the phone to me.

"Mike," I said, "we've got to see you. It's very important. Can you come over to Sherman's?"

After we filled the ducks' dish with clean water, Sherman and I sat on the front steps to wait.

About twenty minutes later, Mike came walking up the driveway. I hadn't stopped to think that, even with a license, he might not be able to use one of the family cars any time he wanted.

Sherman and I took him around back to the duck cage.

"Colonel Fairbrook gave them to my parents," Sherman said.

Mike watched the ducks. "Fairbrook. He's the guy who owns . . ."

"Half the county," Sherman said. "He gave them to my folks to eat. It's going to happen a few days after Thanksgiving."

Mike looked at Sherman closely. "Did you talk to your folks?"

"Oh, yes." Sherman's voice was low. "The ducks are going to be killed. The thing is, you can't have two ducks hanging around your yard, you can't get to know them, and then just let them be killed."

"You know the lake out by the junior college?" I'd been thinking about that lake even before we called Mike. "There are flocks of geese and ducks there— plain white ducks, too, so these guys wouldn't even stand out. Only, there's no way Sherman and I could carry two ducks across town, even if they'd let us, without being noticed. And they sure wouldn't sit in a coaster wagon."

"What if your parents caught you?" Mike asked Sherman.

"They always sleep late Sunday. I figured, if we do it very early. . . ."

"We who?" Mike asked.

"You could park on the street," I said. "The hedges would hide you from the house. If you heard loud voices or anything, you could drive away. Sherman and I would say we were letting the ducks out to stretch their legs."

Mike let out a deep breath. "If I do this, neither of you will ask me for another favor as long as you live, okay?"

I would have hugged him—but he was sixteen, after all.

Six

I woke my father the next morning to tell him I was going over to Sherman's.

"Wha . . . what time is it?" He groped for his glasses.

"Pretty early. I'll be back in a couple of hours at the most."

Before he could wake enough to ask more questions, I left.

I had enough questions of my own to torment me. Considering that the house we lived in was rented from Sherman's parents, who were not at all pleased to have us there, was I betraying my family by taking the risk of liberating the ducks? I reminded myself again that if we were caught, we could say we were just letting them out for a little exercise.

Mike was parked a few yards before Sherman's driveway, in his family's station wagon. By now, I was feeling so paranoid I didn't even wave to him.

Sherman was waiting by the side of his house, shivering in his jeans and windbreaker.

As we crept around to the back, I could feel the toast I'd wolfed earlier coming up in my throat.

Sherman lifted the top of the cage.

The ducks huddled together in the corner.

"Wait. Wait," I whispered. "If we try to grab them, and they start quacking . . ."

"I read somewhere that if you throw a cloth over a bird it quiets down," Sherman ventured.

"Why didn't you think of that sooner?" I wasn't all that convinced about the cloth deal, but I was getting more and more scared we'd be caught with the ducks in the pale dawn, and the "giving them a little exercise" excuse was beginning to sound unbelievable even to me.

"Shall I get a blanket?"

"No. No, Sherman, don't go back in the house again! Why don't we try this another time when we have blankets?"

"Just a second." Sherman took off his windbreaker and dropped it into the cage, covering one duck and the rear of the other.

The duck covered by the jacket didn't even struggle as Sherman picked him up.

It was too late to back out. We couldn't stand there, Sherman holding a duck in a windbreaker, Mike parked near the driveway. The longer we stayed around, the more likely we were to be caught—and we couldn't look much more suspicious than we did now.

I took off my coat and tossed it at the second duck. It landed over his back and head. As I grabbed him, he let out a muffled, anxious quack, but he didn't struggle when I wrapped my coat around him.

Clutching the ducks to us, Sherman and I ran, bent over like a couple of SWAT team hotshots.

Even before we reached the car, Mike was holding the back door open. I piled in first, then Sherman, and then Mike got in and pulled away, not even burning rubber, which must have taken a lot of control.

He glanced in the rearview mirror. "You *disguised* them?"

"It's to calm them." I glanced around at the deserted street.

"You'd better uncover their heads so they get enough air," he advised. "But hang on to them. I haven't been driving long enough to handle a couple of ducks flying around in the car."

I felt nervous easing my coat off the duck's head, but there was no point rescuing a bird and then half smothering it. "Okay, duck, I'm your friend. I'm trying to save your life here." Carefully, I worked my coat back from the top of his head, his eyes, then his bill. He didn't even quack at me but sat, patient and resigned, or maybe kind of stunned, looking around him.

I was beginning to feel fond of this duck.

Sherman, too, had got his bird's head free.

I don't know whether the ducks sensed that we were saving them or whether being wrapped in clothes did calm them—or confuse them—but they sat quietly as we drove through town.

We three humans were quiet, too. I wondered whether Mike would have agreed to help us if he had taken time to picture this rescue. I was even more scared than I'd been in Sherman's yard. What if a cruising police car spotted a sixteen-year-old driving around at seven-thirty on a Sunday morning, with two ducks, one wearing a coat and another a windbreaker, sitting on the laps of two kids in the backseat?

When we passed a couple of joggers, both Sherman and I instantly huddled over our ducks.

The road to the junior college was empty. We parked right before a little bridge, overlooking the lake.

Mike got out of the car and steadied me and then Sherman as we climbed out, carrying the ducks.

It was a lovely area, with big trees all around and grassy banks leading down to the shore. On the lake, dozens of geese and ducks were swimming lazily.

As we started down the slope, some of the ducks headed toward us, quacking, thinking we were bringing treats, I guess.

That's all it took. My duck started quacking back, paddling with his feet, straining to move his wings.

The bank was slick from winter damp. As my bird struggled to get to the lake, my feet slid out from under me, and I slid down the bank on my back, still holding him.

By the time we hit the bottom of the slope, he was half out of the coat, one wing flapping wildly. Still on my back, I pulled the rest of the coat off him, flinching from those flailing wings.

Balancing his rush with outstretched wings, he ran into the water, then swam right past the crowd paddling toward me.

A minute later, Sherman's duck waddled down the bank and into the lake.

"You all right?" Sherman squatted beside me, holding his windbreaker.

"I think so."

Mike picked up my coat.

My clothes were damp, and there were feathers all over my coat, but we stood and watched for a few minutes. All the birds were swimming around together now, as if our two had always been part of the flock.

"You're going to be in for some heavy questioning when your folks realize those ducks are gone," Mike told Sherman as we got into the car. "And you'll be in serious trouble if they find out you took them."

Sherman shook a few feathers off his jacket before he shut the door.

Mike didn't even mention anybody else being in

trouble. He knew, as I did, that Sherman would never tell who had helped him, no matter what.

And I thought that even if somehow I did get found out, it would be worth it—except for my family. When it came to getting my family in trouble, I was not so sure.

But I had a feeling that if I had it to do again, I'd risk it.

When I got home, I shook out my coat again, and then slipped in the back door. "Hi! Here I am!" I called, and hurried to the bathroom to clean up before my father could spot me.

By now I was feeling even more anxious. Sherman's parents would know an eleven-year-old kid could never have made off with those ducks alone.

Maybe they'd think somebody else had done it, and not Sherman at all!

But I didn't even have time for relief to sink in before another thought hit me. *What if they thought somebody else had taken the ducks, and called the police?*

What if the newspapers got the story?

Even if I was never caught, would I ever stop being afraid I might be?

I went into the bathroom and showered, wondering what was happening to Sherman.

Normally, Mrs. Farisee took weekends off. But this Sunday, after church, she changed from her flowered polyester dress and black pumps into a dark blue shirtdress and brown oxfords. Then she began organizing.

She strode into the parlor, where my father was reading the Sunday paper. "Is there any kind of decent tablecloth anywhere in this house?"

Putting the paper down, he edged behind the Hide-A-Bed and opened the cedar chest. The twins stood beside the sofa, fascinated and silent. I squatted beside my father, taking the things he pulled out of the chest and piling them on the rug.

You never get tired of seeing items that are stored away out of sight in trunks and basements and attics. Since you're not allowed to paw through them ordinarily, you don't get to see old family treasures that often. It almost took my mind off what my ducknapping might have brought down on all of us.

My father unearthed a tablecloth and napkins from near the bottom of the chest. That white damask tablecloth must have been in the family longer than I'd been alive. There were seven matching napkins. Before our mother left, whenever I set the table on a holiday, I wondered what had happened to the eighth napkin. Each time I asked, and each time my father gave me a different tale: It had been eaten by a grizzly that had come right through the back door, attracted by the cooking smells. My mother's great-granduncle had tied it to a broom and used it as a flag of surrender when he fought in the Civil War.

I handed the cloth and the napkins to Mrs. Farisee, who looked at the cloth impassively, and then counted the napkins.

"Seven," she said.

Of course, my father could hardly tell her a grizzly had eaten the eighth. "Just right," he said.

"They'll have to be laundered," she declared. "And by hand. They'd never stand up to a machine."

He stood. "You want me to . . ."

"Heavens, no," she told him. "You have to know what you're doing when you handle fine fabrics."

Mrs. Farisee took the linens into the kitchen, and the twins went after her.

It took a while to put back the things my father had taken out of the chest. Normally, I would have looked everything over before I handed it to him, but today I had the duck episode on my mind. Besides, seeing the damask tablecloth again, I couldn't help thinking about Thanksgivings when my mother was home.

After everything was put away, my father picked up the Sunday paper and settled down on the sofa again. I think the tablecloth had gotten to him, too.

I went into the kitchen. There was no way of knowing how long I had to wait to know what the fallout from the duck caper would be. The only way to get through the suspense was to stay busy and keep my mind on other things.

Mrs. Farisee had the tablecloth and napkins soaking in the sink.

"Tomorrow," she said, "we'll polish the silver. It's a ragtag collection, but when silver doesn't match, it looks as if it's been in the family for generations."

"I think most of it did come from our grandmothers," I told her. "Somewhere back along the line, they must have been complete sets."

"Things happen," she said. "I remember once when I was a girl my father put all our sterling silver flatware in boiling water in an aluminum pan."

Even Aida, who had no respect for sterling silver, was impressed. *"Why?"*

"It was supposed to soak the tarnish off. When the water cooled, he went to fish out the flatware, and all this black goo had come out of the knife handles, along with the blades. He put the blades and handles in a bag, meaning to get them soldered together again, but my mother thought the bag was trash and threw it out."

With her confiding like that, I couldn't help but volunteer a confession of my own. "Over the years, I've dropped three sterling spoons into the garbage disposal. You don't notice until you turn it on and hear them, and you know right away what you've done."

"I remember the time we used our big silver spoon to dig a grave for our goldfish," Antony told Mrs. Farisee. "Boy, did we get yelled at."

"You can't dig a good grave with spoons anyway," Aida observed. "They bend."

"Enough about graves." Mrs. Farisee sat down at

the kitchen table. "The next thing to do is to make a list."

"Of what?" Aida asked.

"A grocery list," Mrs. Farisee told her. "First we decide on our menu, and then we write down what we need to buy."

Aida had no interest in lists, so she wandered back to the bedroom she shared with Antony and me.

Antony was delighted to help plan what we'd eat. Rather than argue with him, Mrs. Farisee and I simply overlooked suggestions like cherry sodas and cheese dogs and corn chips.

What surprised me was that Mrs. Farisee got so involved. Then I realized that Thanksgiving dinner, even if it was with a family that wasn't her own, meant a lot to her.

She had written *turkey* at the top of her list, without anybody mentioning it.

After she put down the pencil, I said, "How about if we don't have turkey?"

She looked at me without speaking.

"Let me put it this way. I would just like you to spare a turkey, in the spirit of the season."

Mrs. Farisee wasn't upset. "You get a choice."

"Oh, good!" I tried to think of some vegetarian main dishes.

"Turkey or ham," she said.

After dinner, Mike Harbinger's little brother Preston telephoned Antony. Usually, Antony went home with Preston or brought Preston to our house after kindergarten two or three times a week. I tensed up, until I was convinced that Preston wasn't telling Antony that Mike had been apprehended for ducknapping.

Still, I kept listening to my brother talking on the phone in the hallway.

"I can't," he said. "I've got to come right home from school. We've got to go grocery shopping. I'll probably be busy until Thanksgiving."

The kid sounded like an executive with an overcrowded calendar. Could Thanksgiving dinner be that important to a five-year-old? I wondered. Maybe. Maybe, to a five-year-old whose mother had walked out on him.

Seven

Monday morning, Sherman showed up earlier than he ever had, but I was already at the back door, holding Antony by the hand.

The minute we were out of the yard, I asked, "So?"

"The maid went out to feed the ducks this morning and came back in to ask my parents where they were. My father went out to look for them, and I left for your house."

That meant we had hours to wait until Sherman was questioned. But I didn't say anything. There was no point in making both of us suffer any more than we were.

Laurelle got to the storeroom just a few minutes after Sherman and me.

I was grateful for having the posters to take my mind off the ducknapping. Even now, neither Sherman nor I mentioned it to Laurelle. It wasn't that I didn't trust her, it was just that liberating those ducks was something so serious and terrifying that I couldn't bring myself to tell anybody who hadn't been part of it.

The three of us met in the storeroom at lunch to finish the posters.

Laurelle unwrapped a peanut-butter sandwich. "I talked to my mother last night. I told her maybe I was going to stop eating meat."

"What did she say?" I took out my own peanut-butter sandwich.

"She wanted to know how I was going to get enough protein."

"That's what everybody who's nervous about vegetarians asks," Sherman said. "Most people in this country get more protein than they need, and when you get too much protein, your body starts losing calcium."

I watched him open his lunch. "I just want to know how to get enough protein without living on peanut butter for the rest of my life. What's in your sandwich?"

He began eating with his right hand and painting with his left. "Tofu and tahini with lettuce and Bermuda onion. I made it myself. You don't want to eat too much peanut butter. Some of it may have aflatoxins."

An incredibly brilliant person can drive you crazy.

"Sherman!" I cried.

"Okay, so protein. You've got high-protein grains like amaranth and triticale and quinoa . . ."

Laurelle and I looked at each other blankly.

"Amaranth? Triticale? Quinoa?" I repeated.

"All the health food stores have them," he said. "And you can get plenty of protein foods in any grocery store—beans, nuts, sunflower seeds, sprouts, tofu . . . you can do anything with tofu. Listen, I'll bring you some vegetarian cookbooks. I bought them for my parents, but we've never had a maid who'd look at one."

At the end of the hour, we had the last poster finished. "Neat." Laurelle gazed at our work with satisfaction. "We have a makeup rehearsal after school, but we can post them tomorrow."

"Fine," I said.

"I'll ask Razi to give me a requisition to get what we need to put them up. He'll be impressed that I'm working on the publicity committee too. Poor Razi. Lars Svenson absolutely refuses to wear mascara. Teena is having a fit. I mean, a King of Siam with blond eyelashes is pretty unauthentic. I have to admit, though, I'm kind of relieved I don't get stuck with trying to put mascara on him."

After school, Aida and I walked partway home with Sherman. A few blocks from his house we all slowed down. "I'll see you tomorrow," he said, and walked on alone. I could tell he didn't want us to come any farther.

I didn't dare telephone him that evening. All I could do was wait and wonder what was happening to him.

Aida was still in her pajamas when Sherman arrived the next morning.

"I get to go grocery shopping!" she announced.

" 'S not fair." Antony had been grumbling " 'S not fair" since before breakfast.

Mrs. Farisee unbuttoned his coat and buttoned it properly. "I know it's not fair, but I am not taking a pair of five-year-olds grocery shopping just before Thanksgiving. One is all I can handle. And I am not going to go in the afternoon, and struggle through the crowds. If you behave yourself and stop growling, I may consider letting you polish the silver."

I think Antony felt he should keep grumping, just on principle, but he was afraid of losing the honor of polishing silver, so he merely scowled and kept quiet.

The minute we got out the back door, I asked Sherman, "Well?"

"It was interesting," he said.

"Interesting! Sherman!"

Antony stopped scowling and settled down, since nobody was paying any attention to him.

"My father was at a meeting, and my mother was at her aerobics class," Sherman went on, "so they didn't get home until dinnertime."

"They didn't just forget about the ducks?"

"Oh, no. My mother said the maid had probably left the top of the cage open after she fed them Saturday. My father agreed. Then he said he'd have to buy two more, since the colonel wouldn't see them until after they were cooked."

I felt just totally sick and defeated. We saved two ducks, so two more were going to die.

"Then my father decided maybe the ducks hadn't got out of the cage by themselves. Before long he talked himself into being sure they'd been ripped off."

"Oh, boy." There was worse to come, I realized.

"He even called the newspapers, and the TV station in the city."

I was stunned. "He turned you in?"

"No, no, no, Dez. My dad said, 'The media covered the story when the ducks were given to us. They have to cover the story of them being stolen.' Candidates will do anything to get their names in the paper, Dez. So my father is getting more free publicity."

"Wait. You mean he's *happy* the ducks were stolen?"

"He's delighted. My mother isn't exactly downcast, either. Now she doesn't have to worry how to get the ducks slaughtered. 'It was either all the blood and the scene in our backyard, which I'm sure is against some ordinance,' she said, 'or it was transporting them somewhere where they do things like that.' Also, she wasn't looking forward to overseeing another fancy dinner right after Thanksgiving. They're taking the colonel to a restaurant, and she made my father promise not to let him give us any more ducks. You know what she said? She said, 'Tell him Sherman gets too fond of them.' "

I had been living with the fear of what would happen for so long I still felt haunted. "Sherman, if they ever find out we did it . . ."

"How? Only three of us know, and none of us will ever tell. Besides, my parents don't *want* to find out. Think how my father would feel, after calling the paper and everything, if he ever had to admit I did it."

He had a point. Still, I knew I would feel uneasy about it . . . until something worse came up.

Laurelle was in the storeroom with a hammer, a box of tacks, and a roll of tape.

"You guys want to see the flier?" Sherman asked.

"You did it! You finished it!" I was so proud of him, working on the flier with all the stress he'd been under, you would have thought he was my brother.

He took a paper out of his binder and put it on the table.

At the top of the page he had pasted two pictures. One was of cows in a feedlot, standing mired to their bellies in mud. The other was of live chickens packed tight in a cage with their beaks cut off. Under it, he had typed a description of how calves and pigs are raised and killed, and after that, *Christmas is a gentle time—this year let the animals live.*

"I could have gotten more pictures," Sherman said.

I studied the flier. "No. This gets the idea across."

"I'm wondering how the people at the play will react," Laurelle muttered. "Of course, I expect it used to annoy plantation owners when people said keeping slaves wasn't nice."

"So you think the flier's okay?" Sherman asked.

"I think it's great," I said.

"Then I'll take it to the copy shop after school."

Laurelle fished ten dollars out of her backpack and gave it to him. I handed him three dollars and sixty cents.

"We ought to get the posters up now," I suggested.

"Not until we talk to Elliot Lofting," she said.

He was in the detention room, sitting at the big table, his back to the glass door. When Sherman and Laurelle and I walked in, Elliot turned around, looking wary, as if we were a tribe from a strange village.

"So. Elliot." Laurelle plopped down on the chair next to his.

Sherman and I sat down across from them.

"How are the programs coming?" Sherman asked.

"Why?" Elliot had lost none of that old charm.

"We finished the posters, and we thought you might need some help."

This did not warm up Elliot. "They're almost done."

Laurelle looked down at the sheet in front of him. "That's neat, Elliot."

"How many pages?" I asked.

"One sheet, but with another blue cover sheet."

"Will you need any help folding them or stapling them?" Sherman asked.

"Razi says they'll do that when they copy them."

"We're putting up posters at lunch," Laurelle said. "Want to help?"

Elliot seemed taken aback, surprised and embarrassed and pleased. "Well . . . sure."

I was beginning to feel uncomfortable stringing him along like this. Turkeys or people, the principle is the same: you don't have to be smart or handsome or charming to deserve being treated decently.

"I suppose you'll be in charge of handing out the programs, since you made them," Laurelle told Elliot.

He looked uncertain. "I thought the ushers did that."

"I think you should be in charge," Laurelle pressed. "How many ushers will there be?"

Elliot frowned. "I don't know. Ten, twelve . . ."

"See?" Sherman said. "Somebody has to keep those kids in line. How about we pass out the programs, while you oversee the ushering."

I knew I couldn't go on with this. "Listen, Elliot." I leaned forward, my elbows on the table. "We are making up some fliers we want to put in the programs. We want to get hold of the programs in time to put our sheets in, and we want to hand them out ourselves."

Sherman and Laurelle looked at me, dumfounded.

"Do you have permission?" Elliot asked.

"No," I said. "And we're not going to ask permission."

"Then you can't . . ."

"Sherman," I said, "show him the flier."

Sherman dug the paper out of his backpack and put it on the table.

Elliot studied it for a couple of minutes. "Why are you going to put this in the play programs?"

"So everybody at the play will see it," I said. "That way, a few people may decide not to eat meat, and a few animals may be saved."

I think Elliot knew there was no good argument against that. "I can't let you put these in the programs without permission."

"We're not asking you to let us," I said. "You don't have to get involved at all. We showed you the fliers, and I'm telling you what we're going to do. We'll take all the responsibility. You could stop us. You could go to Razi or the principal, but I don't think you want to fink on us for trying to save animals."

Elliot handed the flier to Sherman. "I'm not going to have anything to do with it."

"That's all we ask," I said.

Laurelle stood up. "I'll tell Razi that you're going to supervise the ushers, and Sherman and Dez will hand out the programs."

"You're on the makeup committee," Elliot reminded her.

"Yeah, but I know him better than Dez and Sherman do," Laurelle said. "And anybody trying to direct dozens of junior high school kids in a play is going to welcome anybody's offering to take on any responsibility."

Elliot still looked dubious. "When the teachers find out about those fliers . . ."

"They'll ask the people who handed them out. And we'll tell them it was all our idea, and that nobody else had anything to do with it," Sherman assured him.

"Because I won't have anything to do with it." Elliot was firm.

As Sherman and Laurelle and I started to leave, I looked down at his programs. "They really do look good, Elliot."

"Do you still want me to help put up posters?" he asked.

It was fun at lunchtime, putting the rest of the play posters up in the halls and the cafeteria. We got a ladder from Mr. Hofstaeder, and each of us took a turn on the ladder while the other three steadied it and called up directions. Naturally, a lot of kids stopped to watch, and ask questions, and make dumb remarks.

I felt almost like a celebrity.

As for Elliot, I suspect it was the best day he'd ever had at school. He smiled a couple of times, and gave the person on the ladder a lot of advice, and put up the final poster himself, and even volunteered to return the ladder to Mr. Hofstaeder.

By the time Sherman and I went to pick up Aida, I'd almost forgotten I was a ducknapper.

Eight

My sister was standing on the corner by her school with her friend Tran Luan and Tran's mother, sobbing. When a little kid cries hard without making much noise, you know her heart is broken.

"The dogs," Tran told me in a scared and breathless voice. "Your dogs are gone."

I squatted in front of Aida.

It was hard to talk, as if speaking about it made it be true. But I asked, with the notion that maybe Tran had gotten it all wrong. "Aida, what happened?"

My sister took a couple of shuddering breaths.

I felt Sherman's hand on my shoulder. "We'd better start for your house while she tells us," he said.

"Shall we come?" Tran asked.

"That's okay," Sherman said. "We can handle it."

Sherman always comes through in an emergency. Besides, it was a cold day with a sharp wind, and

Mrs. Luan had been kneeling there in her thin coat and slacks, trying to comfort my sister.

It took six blocks, walking as fast as Aida could keep up with us, before Sherman and I got the whole story. Aida had gone to the store with Mrs. Farisee, leaving the dogs in the backyard. When they got home, Herb and Joe and Sadie were gone.

A whitewashed, four-foot-tall, flat-top picket fence enclosed our backyard. Usually when we came home, we could see Herb and Joe and Sadie standing with their paws on the top rail, wagging and barking. They'd never tried to jump the fence. We'd always figured that, with the three of them, they had so much going on in their own yard, they felt no need to leave it.

Hurrying home, I was furious at my father and Mrs. Farisee for not thinking that, if the dogs could get over the fence, some day they would. Then I felt guilty because I hadn't nagged my father into building a taller fence.

Our station wagon was parked outside our house. Mrs. Farisee was in the kitchen. "I'll stay by the phone," she told us. "I've called the police and the SPCA and all the veterinary hospitals." She handed me a dozen sheets of paper and two rolls of tape. On the papers was printed with a red marking pen DOGS LOST, then descriptions of the three dogs, our home phone number, and our father's office number.

"Stick these up wherever you can," she said. "Meanwhile I'll print up something neater, and we can get copies made. Your father is out looking with Antony. Aida, you stay here and warm up."

Aida shook her head, sending tears skidding almost sideways across her face. "I want to go find the dogs."

Mrs. Farisee looked sharply at my sister. "All right. But you stay with Desdemona and Sherman every second."

"Will you call my house and tell the maid I'm helping to search for the dogs?" Sherman asked Mrs. Farisee. "You may have to explain a few times."

She nodded. "You stay right together," she ordered. "And I want you back here before five. I'm too old to worry about beasts and children all at once."

I held Aida's hand, and we walked on the opposite side of the street from Sherman, all of us peering down alleys and into yards, calling and whistling, sticking Mrs. Farisee's posters on light posts and fences, not even caring if we got in trouble for it.

When we saw anybody on the street, Sherman would ask, "Have you seen three big shaggy dogs?"

Nobody had.

I was half afraid somebody would say yes and try to lure us to go with him, and then we'd have to run and call the police, which would slow down our looking for the dogs.

After walking about a quarter of an hour, I saw my father coming toward us, carrying Antony.

"I have to take him home," my father told me when they got closer. "He's walked out. I've already checked the parks. You try the schools. The dogs would tend to hang around kids. You stick right together, and stay out in the open until I come back with the car. Meet me at the high school football field at five. Wait there if I'm late. Sherman, do your folks know . . ."

"Oh, yes. Mrs. Farisee called them." Sherman squinted at his watch. "I make it four thirty-two. . . ."

My father glanced at his own watch. "Fine. I'll call your parents again and tell them I'll drive you home before dark."

Sherman looked worried. "What if we haven't found the dogs?"

"Dez and I will keep looking until we do," my father promised. "Meet you at the field." He walked away, Antony clinging to him.

Sherman and Aida and I turned down the street to our right. "You know," Sherman said quietly, "he won't get much sympathy from my folks. They think a family with three dogs that aren't even purebred ought to be living in a chicken coop, or an abandoned car."

The schoolyards and even the high school football field were deserted. The winter sun was low and watery, and there seemed to be a space all around us where no sound penetrated.

Everything seems worse as the daylight fades. I wondered how I'd live through the next hours, and days, and weeks, if we didn't find the dogs.

We walked up and down side streets, and finally

we came to the place where Sherman's family was putting up condominiums. The concrete had been poured, a whole city block of flat, wet gray. There were five workmen still there, setting sawhorses and Do Not Enter signs around the edges of the slab.

"Maybe they came by here." Sherman walked toward the men.

Then he started running.

I saw them too. The dogs were on the other side of that great stretch of concrete, trotting along, jaunty and excited.

Aida snatched her hand from mine. "Dogs!" She darted toward them—right into the concrete. She was so thrilled to see the animals, she kept struggling forward.

"Aida!" I plunged after her.

The men began yelling. "Hey! Hey! Hey!"

Herb and Joe and Sadie came galloping to greet us.

"No! Stop! Stay!" I screamed.

But the dogs were too excited to listen. When they hit the concrete, they kept laboring toward us.

The men, of course, didn't want to wade into the wet slab they'd just poured, so they ran around the edges, shouting at us.

I didn't know how long it would be before that stuff hardened completely, but I realized that if we stopped moving we could be cemented right into the foundation.

100

"Back! Back!" I yelled at the dogs as I slogged after my sister.

Sherman, good old loyal Sherman, was right with me.

Floundering in concrete, with us screaming "Back!" at them, and strange men yelling threats and curses, the poor dogs were so confused they stood still for a second.

"No! No!" I realized that if they didn't move, they would surely be stuck. "Don't stop!" If they could make it to Sherman and me, somehow we'd drag them free.

By now, the workmen were in an awful state, screaming and stamping and throwing things down on the ground in a rage.

Wet concrete sucks at your feet, thicker than swamp mud or quicksand, so that every step is a great, great effort.

Luckily, Aida had been slowed down, too. I got close enough to grab her hand. Sherman seized her other hand. We yanked her up out of the muck, and then he and I managed to turn, hauling her between us with her feet dragging the concrete, and wade back toward the edge of the slab.

Our old station wagon pulled up, and my father leaped out.

The workmen yelled even louder to see a grown man run onto the concrete.

Sherman and I strained forward. With a great

heave, we lifted my sister as my father reached out his arms.

As he snatched her up, she closed her arms around his neck.

The dogs had fought their way to us. I got my hand under Herb's collar. Sherman grabbed Joe's. My father put Aida down and got hold of Sadie.

The workmen were all at our edge of the slab by now. I guess they realized that having four people and three dogs stuck in their foundation would be a serious problem. One took Aida from my father, and the others helped pull the rest of us free.

"Water!" My father held Aida close.

One of the workmen picked up Sherman. Another ran to a water outlet a few feet away and turned it on.

My father put Aida down and washed as much concrete off her feet as he could while the water spilled over them—the concrete had sucked both Aida's shoes and one of mine clean off us. While my father washed my foot, Sherman scraped the concrete off his own shoes with a stick.

Then we grabbed the dogs, one by one, and rinsed off their paws. Finally, my father hit his shoes against the water pipe, knocking chunks of concrete off them.

In the fading light, we all began to look as gray as that great stretch of foundation. I could barely make out three shoes standing empty in the scarred slab.

The workmen had gone from fury to helpfulness,

but now they seemed tired and confused. One put his jacket over me, and one put his over Sherman. My father wrapped Aida in his suit coat and lifted her. "I've got to get these kids home."

"Wait a minute." The man who'd put his jacket over me straightened up. "Do you realize the damage those dogs and kids have done?"

"I'll be responsible." My father sounded very tired.

"If my crew tried to go in there now, they'd be stuck fast. We're going to have to wait until that slab dries so we can get in there and break those shoes out. Do you know what that's going to do to the slab—to say nothing of all those footprints? This . . . this . . . gang has made a Swiss cheese out of . . ."

"I know." Taking my hand and carrying Aida, my father started for the car.

I barely managed to take off the jacket and hand it to its owner.

Sherman returned the other jacket and hurried after us.

The dogs trotted beside and behind and in front of us, trying to be as close to their people as possible.

The man who had been talking to my father kept up with him, dodging around the dogs. "And who are you?"

My father didn't slow down. "I'm the man who'll be responsible."

"Listen, wise guy . . ." The man was getting angrier, but you don't grab a father who is carrying one child and leading another. Not when the father's three dogs are with him.

Sadie swerved to throw a shoulder block at the man. At the same time Herb and Joe whirled to face him.

The man stopped.

My father and Sherman and I hurried on. At the car, my father called, "Come!" and the dogs ran to us. None of the men followed.

Herb and Joe and Sadie clambered into the car, delighted to be getting a ride on top of all the other thrills they'd had. It had been, for them, a day of great adventures—travel, amazing experiences, meeting new people, and a chance to be brave and noble protectors of the family.

Of course, they didn't know they had just ruined the family.

I sat up front with Aida. As Sherman climbed into the backseat, the dogs tumbled all over each other, trying to sit on him, kissing him, yelping as they got stepped on by the other dogs.

"We got your license number, turkey!" one of the men yelled as we pulled away.

My father turned on the heater. "I'd better get you right home," he told Sherman. "I'll come in and explain what happened."

"I don't think you could." Sherman was shivering, but his voice was calm. "This is more complicated than you can get across to our maid in English."

We rode in silence for a few minutes, except for

the slurping and chewing noises of the dogs trying to get the remaining concrete off their paws.

"What am I going to tell my folks in the morning?" Sherman asked.

"The truth," my father said.

Sherman sighed. "When you called my house, did you by any chance mention to the maid that I was helping to look for your three dogs?"

"I told your mother."

"She was home?" Sherman asked.

"She and your father were getting ready to go to a reception. They said to get you home by dark."

Sherman sounded resigned but depressed. "So you told her we were looking for your dogs. And those workmen will sure tell them about the three dogs and the three kids who ran through the concrete. I guess there was still enough light for them to get a good look at us—and they said they got your license number." He was quiet for a minute. "It's too bad kids can't take the Fifth."

For the first time that afternoon, my father seemed to relate to something besides his children and the dogs and what they'd brought down on him. "Where did you learn that, Sherman?"

"In some book about government. The Fifth Amendment to the Constitution says you can't be forced to testify against yourself. You can say, 'I respectfully decline to answer on the grounds that such testimony might tend to incriminate me.' "

"Sherman." My father almost smiled. "Nothing you

say could incriminate you. You were trying to get Aida and the dogs out of wet concrete."

"Yeah, but what about the concept of waiver?" Sherman still seemed anxious.

"What is he talking about?" I wondered if we were in even more trouble than I thought.

"Waiver," my father told me. "If a person who's called to testify answers any questions, beyond his name, address, neutral stuff, if he answers any questions that have to do with the matter under discussion, he waives the right to refuse to answer any further questions. In other words, he gives up the right."

"What does this have to do with . . ."

"I mean I don't want to fink on you guys," Sherman said.

When we got to Sherman's house, my father went in with him, and came back in just a minute.

"Did you explain?" I asked.

He started the car. "Their maid was on the telephone. She didn't want to be interrupted."

As we pulled up in front of our house, I saw the porch light was on.

"Dez," my father said, "go in and get the leashes."

As I got to the front door, Mrs. Farisee opened it, Antony right beside her.

"You've got them! You've got them!" he yelled.

Mrs. Farisee had the leashes on the table by the door.

She handed me one and grabbed Antony's arm as he tried to dash toward the wagon.

Mrs. Farisee does have a way with dogs. Herb and Joe and Sadie were crying and clawing at the door to get at Antony, and then she looked in the window.

"Sit!" she commanded. "Stay!"

The dogs sat as if their hindquarters had suddenly collapsed.

Opening the car door, she snapped a leash on Herb's collar, and another on Joe's. "Come!" she ordered.

They were still crying with excitement, but quietly. Herb and Joe stepped out of the wagon and licked Antony, but didn't even try to put their paws on his shoulders.

I leashed Sadie. She jumped out of the car, baying.

"You!" Mrs. Farisee pointed at her.

Sadie sat down on the sidewalk and offered her a paw.

Antony threw his arms around Sadie, who kissed him, sincerely but politely.

My father got out with Aida.

"Well," Mrs. Farisee said. "You're going to have to settle for a slapdash supper. You all go wash up. I'll feed the animals first."

"What we have to do first," my father told her, "is get the concrete out from between their toes."

I held each dog still while my father, nose to claws, cut off chunks of concrete and hair with a manicure scissors, all the time growling, "Get out of my light!" "Don't *lean* on me!" and "Stop breathing in my ear!" at the twins.

After Aida and I showered, he took a long bath. My sister and I spent some time sitting on our bedroom floor, picking bits of concrete from between our toes, while she told Antony what had happened.

At dinner, she told the whole story over again for Mrs. Farisee. I could tell my father didn't want to hear it, but I think he was too tired to object.

After the dishes were done and the twins in bed, I came out to the parlor. My father was sitting on the sofa. The television was off, and he wasn't reading or doing paperwork. When your parent just sits like that, looking at nothing, you realize how beat down he feels.

"What do you think will happen?" I asked him.

"I don't know." He put his arm around me. "I'll call Sherman's parents in the morning."

Nine

My father was at the table when the twins and I went into the kitchen the next morning. After I kissed him, I asked, "Have you had time to call the Groves yet?"

"Honey," he told me, "the worst time to talk business to anybody is before breakfast. I'll phone him from work later this morning."

"What are we going to do about keeping the dogs home? Now that they know they can get out, they're going to do it again. They had a wonderful time out on the streets."

"I'll pick up some lumber after work and make the fence higher."

"Will the Groves let you?"

"I should think so, if I'm paying for it."

When he finished breakfast, he got up and hugged Aida and then Antony and then me. "Don't worry," he said.

How can a person with nothing but trouble *not* worry?

Right after my father left for work, Sherman showed up. He looked pale, and his eyes were blood-shot.

Mrs. Farisee eyed him closely. "Are you coming down with something?"

"No, ma'am," he said. "I didn't sleep very well."

Antony spent so much time hugging the dogs good-bye, I had to yell at him that he was making us late. He got the front of his coat covered with dog hair, so we had to wait while Mrs. Farisee brushed it. She promised him she'd let the dogs stay in the house until he got home.

"So?" I asked Sherman as we left the house.

"I don't know. My folks weren't up yet when I left this morning. I was glad. I didn't want to be around when they hear about the concrete."

"Boy, Sherman." I shook my head. "It seems as if lately all we do is wait to find out how terrible the trouble we're in is going to be."

"Yeah. I've had a stomachache all morning."

Antony had delayed us enough so that we ran into Mike and Preston and their friends.

Preston started talking as if he were continuing a conversation he and Antony had broken off only minutes earlier, telling him all about how his father had promised him a two-wheeler for Christmas.

Mike looked at Sherman intently. "Are you all right?"

"Just tired," Sherman said.

Antony waited for Preston to draw a breath, then announced, "Our dogs ran through Sherman's folks' concrete yesterday, and my sisters' shoes are still stuck in the concrete!"

That quieted even Preston. The kindergartners walked in a cluster around my brother as he told them the whole story.

"Are the dogs all right?" Mike asked me.

I nodded.

He turned to Sherman. "Are your folks upset about . . . anything else?"

Sherman shook his head. "No. The concrete is enough, though."

Laurelle was waiting outside our school when Sherman and I got there. "When will the copies be done?" she greeted us. Then she stared at Sherman. "You look *horrible!*"

He was even paler than when we'd left the house, and his forehead was damp.

"I couldn't take the flier to the copy shop yesterday." He seemed to have trouble getting his breath.

"What is that sound?" Laurelle demanded.

I heard it, too. "Sherman, you're wheezing."

"You've got to see the nurse," Laurelle said.

He hesitated. "I just . . ."

"She's right." I took him by the arm.

The nurse's station was in the basement, between the cafeteria and the gym.

I'd only seen Ms. Dettweiler, the school nurse, once

before. She was a square-built, square-jawed woman of about forty who wore white polyester pantsuits. The thing that tended to undermine my confidence in her was that her clothes smelled of cigarette smoke.

She was dumping some dead flowers out of a glass tumbler into the sink when we walked in. She didn't look at us. "Yeah?"

Sherman coughed, finishing up with a long, whistling wheeze.

Ms. Dettweiler set the glass on the counter. "Go on back there and stash your stuff, take off your coat and shoes, and sit down on the cot."

"Back there" was separated from the front section of the room by a partition that didn't reach to the ceiling.

Sherman walked around the partition, and Ms. Dettweiler got a thermometer off a shelf over a metal table and went after him. Laurelle and I stood waiting. I was beginning to feel scared that Sherman was seriously sick.

Ms. Dettweiler came back to the front section. "Do either of you know his phone number?"

I gave her his number. While she dialed, I asked, "Is he going to be all right?"

She put her hand over the mouthpiece. "Sure. But the kid needs a doctor. You two better go on to class."

I hesitated. "Is it pneumonia or anything?"

"What's his last name?"

"Grove," Laurelle said.

Ms. Dettweiler turned her attention to the telephone. "Mrs. Grove? This is . . . Well, may I speak to her, please."

The bell rang and Ms. Dettweiler covered the mouthpiece again. "Go along."

"Is it okay if I come back and see how he is?" I asked.

She nodded.

Laurelle tugged at my sleeve, and we left.

After my first class, I went down to the nurse's station.

"His mother came for him," Ms. Dettweiler told me. "He'll be fine. Oh, he left this for you." She gave me a ten-dollar bill, a five, three ones, and sixty cents, plus a sheet of notebook paper, folded like a business letter. On my way to my next class, I opened it. Inside was the flier Sherman had made.

Between worrying about Sherman, and what his parents would do about the concrete, I had no appetite. But I went down to the cafeteria, figuring Laurelle would be there.

She was sitting at a table with a lot of other girls, but when she saw me come in, she waved, then got up and moved to an empty table. I guess, being in a conspiracy with me, she figured we might have details of the plot to talk over.

When I sat down next to her, she held out a pita bread filled with sprouts and something brown. "Falafel. It's neat. Have a bite."

I shook my head and opened my lunch so that she wouldn't coax me to try falafel.

"I was just at the nurse's station," Laurelle said. "Sherman's mother came and got him."

"I went by, too. He left the flier for us. I'll take it to a copy shop after school." I figured it was only fair, since she was going out on a limb talking to Mr. Razi.

"Ms. Dettweiler says he'll be okay, that it just sounds like bronchitis to her." Laurelle tore open a bag of chips and offered it to me.

"No, thanks."

"They're organic—fried in vegetable oil."

"I'm not very hungry."

Laurelle looked worried. "Are you coming down with something, too?"

"No. It's just Sherman being sick, and . . ." I told her about the dogs running through the concrete.

"Oh, wow." She looked truly impressed. "And you just left your shoes in the slab?"

"Yeah."

She shuddered. "Eeyew! What if they decide it's cheaper to leave them than to hack them out, and they just put a floor over them? And then someday another owner decides to put in a new floor, or they tear the building down, and there are those shoes. Can you imagine how grisly?"

It seemed like a shallow reaction, worried as I was about what the Groves would do to us. But I had to admit it was a fascinatingly gruesome idea.

114

Laurelle offered me a carrot stick. I took it, so as not to seem totally negative.

I was too depressed to feel like talking, but I didn't want to just sit there like a lump, so I asked, "What are you doing for Thanksgiving?"

She shrugged. "I guess my mom and my sister and I will make dinner or eat at a restaurant."

I wondered whether her mother was a widow or divorced or just separated, but I thought it would be too personal to ask. Still, it was a relief to meet somebody else who didn't have a standard two-parent home.

"I didn't know what my dad and my brother and sister and I were going to do," I told Laurelle. "But then our housekeeper decided to stay and make dinner for us. My father's invited some woman I don't know, and her *mother*."

"Wow." It was a sincere wow.

"She's not a teenager or anything, but inviting both her and her mother is like he's practically engaged to her, and I've never set eyes on her."

Laurelle broke a cupcake in half and put the larger piece in front of me. "My father's getting married again, to somebody I've never seen. Right after Thanksgiving. My mother had just broken up with the guy she was going out with, and then my father called with his news. I don't know which hit my mom harder. You can tell her mind's not on anything she's doing or saying. My sister and I were going to spend Christmas with my father, but the way he's talking,

I think he's going to weasel out of it to be with his new wife." She shrugged. "It'd be better anyway. It would be awful for my mother to be all alone this Christmas."

"Was he nice?" I took a bite of cupcake.

"Oh, yeah. He calls us when he thinks of us."

"I mean the man your mother was dating."

"His hair was all styled, and he had all this flashy jewelry, and a George Michael suntan. His teeth were so white he must have had them bleached. I just hope she isn't going to keep getting taken in by men like that."

"When my mother walked out on us, my father went through a stage you wouldn't believe. He was dating women who thought 'The Love Connection' was serious documentary television. Then he got some sense. He went out with Pat Troup a few times."

Laurelle looked up. "Pat Troup from the newspaper?"

I nodded.

"She's neat."

"But I don't know what happened. If this other woman is coming to Thanksgiving dinner, he must be serious about her."

Laurelle shook her head. "It's funny. We're at an age when our parents are supposed to be worrying about us, and here we are seeing them through all these stages and crisises. But, listen, the woman your father invited to dinner could be a terrific person."

You never stop to think that a girl who's part of the most popular group in school might have the same problems you do. Talking to Laurelle didn't make me feel any better about Sherman and the concrete and what the fliers would let us in for, but I was beginning to like her more and more.

The minute my last class was over, I picked up Aida.

There were three people in line under the Orders sign in the copy shop, and two under the Pay Here sign. When I got to the head of the orders line, I smoothed out the flier and handed it to the woman behind the counter.

"Regular paper?" She didn't look at me.

"Sure," I said.

She jotted something on a pad. "How many?"

"Eighteen dollars and sixty cents worth, including tax."

She looked at me. "How *many?*"

I was beginning to feel flustered, with people lining up behind me. "Let's see. Four hundred would be twenty dollars. . . ."

"Plus tax," she sighed.

"Okay, how about . . . Make it three hundred and fifty," I said. "How soon will they be ready?"

"You can pick them up Saturday morning."

"Saturday? Isn't there any way to get them sooner?"

"Tomorrow's a holiday." She spoke as if she'd been

reciting the same thing for hours. "And we've got orders piled up."

"But these are very important," I told her.

"They all are. Name?"

"Blank."

She glowered at me.

"That is my name," I said stiffly.

She clipped the order slip to the flier and looked over my head at the person behind me. "Next?"

Walking home, I made my sister promise not to say anything about the fliers. If my father or Mrs. Farisee found out about them, they might forbid me to put them in the programs.

When we got to our front door, Antony was already opening it. I could hear Mrs. Farisee in the kitchen—"Out! Out! Out!"

"She kept us all in," Antony explained. "She said it was too cold for me to stay out back all afternoon, and she was afraid that if I came in without them, the dogs might take a notion to jump the fence again."

I dropped my books on the sofa, and we cut through the parlor and the dining room to check out the smells in the kitchen.

"All the way out!" Mrs. Farisee commanded the dogs, and shut the door to the back porch. Without even turning, she said, "You put your books in your own room, Desdemona, and you both change your clothes before you go out back."

You have to respect somebody who can give orders, and the right ones, without even looking at you.

Aida and I changed our clothes, and then she and Antony went out to wrestle around with the dogs. I watched Mrs. Farisee brush flour off the chopping board into a trash sack.

"The school nurse sent Sherman home," I told her. "He was wheezing."

"I *knew* it. Bad?"

"I don't dare call his house to find out how he is."

She went into the hallway and dialed the telephone.

"This is Mrs. Farisee," she announced. "I'm calling to see how Sherman is."

She listened for a few minutes, then said, "Thank you," and hung up.

By then I was standing beside her.

"The maid says the doctor gave him medicine and told him to stay in bed but promised he'd be 'splendid shortly.' " She fixed me with a suspicious glare. "Why are you clearing your throat?"

"It just feels a little scratchy."

"That's all we need." She marched into the bathroom and came out with a brown bottle. "It's getting to the point I'm tempted to chain a glass in the bathroom." I followed her into the kitchen, where she poured a couple of inches of fizzy colorless liquid into a tumbler. "Gargle with this," she ordered. "But whatever you do, don't swallow!"

"What is it?"

"Peroxide."

The twins came in the back door, followed by the dogs. Mrs. Farisee tore a few paper towels from the roll. "Take off your boots before you come in here," she told the twins, "and then wipe off those dogs' paws."

The telephone rang.

"Get that, Desdemona," Mrs. Farisee told me.

It was my father. "I won't be home until six or six-thirty," he said.

"Did you talk to the Groves?" I didn't want to know, but I had to.

"Yes."

"It's bad, isn't it?"

"About what I expected. I've got to go now, honey."

I hung up, wondering just how much worry a person could take.

I trudged into the kitchen just as Mrs. Farisee was taking a pie from the oven—and just as my brother lifted the glass of peroxide to his lips.

Without even dropping the pie, Mrs. Farisee roared, *"Antony Blank! Put that down!"*

Big-eyed, he set the glass back on the table.

"What is the matter with you?" I snatched up the tumbler.

Mrs. Farisee put the pie on the table. "He's five. When you have been around five-year-olds long enough, you learn that they have a built-in tendency to do things that make no sense whatsoever." She glared at him. "And just what are you doing, starting to drink something that's not yours?"

His lower lip trembled, and his voice was scared. "I thought if nobody wanted it . . ."

"Do you know what is in that glass?" Mrs. Farisee demanded.

"Soda," he whispered.

"Peroxide!" Then she sniffed. "Bother!" She rushed to the oven and took out a second pie, the crust only a little darker than that of the first.

My brother looked at me, awed and scared. *"Rocks' eyes?"*

"Peroxide," I told him. "It's a bleach."

Aida sidled closer, almost as upset as Antony. "What's a bleach?"

Mrs. Farisee set the second pie on the table. "It makes things light."

"It would light up my brother's insides?" Aida looked stricken.

"I don't know what it would do to his insides," I said.

"You must never, never swallow anything you just pick up like that." Mrs. Farisee turned my brother to face her. "If you had drunk that peroxide, we would have had to rush you to the hospital, and they would have had to pump out your stomach."

Pale and thoroughly intimidated, he stared at her.

Aida began to sniffle.

"Take them back to your room," Mrs. Farisee told me. "And take the dogs."

I remembered the telephone call. "That was my dad

on the phone. He won't be home until after six."

"Good," she said. "That will give me time to make myself a cup of tea. Then I am going to my room to lie down with my feet up."

I herded the twins out of the kitchen.

Three dogs and three people make for a crowded bedroom, but the dogs weren't much problem, once I made it clear there was to be no roughhousing on the beds. I tried to do homework. I ordered the twins not to argue above a whisper over which television channel they wanted to watch. Even so, I had too much on my mind to concentrate.

I was almost glad when Mrs. Farisee called me in to help with dinner.

At a quarter past six, the dogs came skidding down the hall into the kitchen and plastered their noses against the door to the dining room, whining.

I went out front to meet my father. He climbed out of the station wagon and hugged me.

"You left the lights on," I reminded him.

"I know. Want to help me unload the car?"

In the back of the wagon were dozens of pieces of lumber.

My father unlocked the tailgate. "When we nail these on, the fence will be six feet high. It may not look great, but it will do for the time we'll be here."

These pieces nailed onto the standing fence would look ridiculous, I thought, but then I realized suddenly what he'd said. "What do you mean, 'for the time we'll be here'?"

"Bring some of the wood."

I climbed into the back of the wagon and collected as much lumber as I thought I could carry. Then I scrambled out with it and went down the driveway after my father.

He put his load of wood over the fence and took mine.

"You'd better tell me what happened," I said.

He started back to the car. "I called the house first, on the chance I'd be able to talk to Mrs. Grove."

"Why?" I hurried to keep up with him.

"I thought I liked her better."

"And?" I prodded.

"She is considerably tougher than her husband."

"Really? She's so . . . pretty, and her voice is so soft. . . ."

"Indeed." He got an armload of wood out of the wagon, then stood waiting for me. "I told her that if they sued me for the few thousand dollars it would cost to repour or repair the concrete, they'd have to spend more than that on legal fees. She said they had an attorney on retainer."

"What does that mean?" I knew of only one kind of retainer. I remember Kerri White crying in the girls' rest room because, after she got her braces taken off, her orthodontist made her wear a retainer. A couple of weeks later, she was cheerful again. She'd left her retainer in a glass of water one night, and in the morning accidentally flushed it down the toilet. At least, she convinced her parents it was an accident. She also managed to convince them that her teeth were straight enough to satisfy anybody but an orthodontist.

My father headed down the driveway with me. "A retainer," he explained, "is a fee you pay an attorney, or an accountant, or anybody like that, just to keep them available for whenever you may need their services." He heaved the wood he carried over the fence, and then took mine and threw it over.

I was feeling more and more uneasy. "So then what did you say?"

"Then I called Harley Grove at his office."

I followed him back to the car. "And?"

"His line was busy."

"Are you trying to torture me? What *happened*?"

"The line was busy, undoubtedly because Mrs. Grove was calling him to fill him in on our conversation. When I finally got through to him, he was all prepared. He had a deal all ready to offer us. An offer . . ."

"Don't say it," I beseeched.

He turned off the car lights and locked the doors, and we walked toward the house. "Here." He took an envelope from his pocket. "Gift certificate for Sherman."

"Why?"

"For new shoes."

Mrs. Farisee opened the front door. "Dinner's all ready, so wash up."

"What was the deal?" I asked my father.

"What deal?" Mrs. Farisee asked.

"If we move out in ninety days, they'll accept seven hundred dollars for the damage to the concrete, and they won't sue us," my father said.

I felt sick. "What did you tell him?"

"Honey, they can afford an attorney. We can't. I'm going to have enough trouble getting seven hundred dollars together." He paused, and then he said, "He made me an offer I couldn't . . ."

"Never mind," I said.

As soon as he finished dinner, my father went out to work on the fence. Even with the light over the back door on and me holding a fluorescent lantern, he missed the nails as often as he hit them.

Mrs. Farisee kept the dogs inside, and at eight she called the twins in to get ready for bed.

A little before ten, my father nailed the last of the wood on the gate. "Well, it's not a thing of beauty, but it'll keep the dogs in. And we have to take it down before we move, anyway."

It wasn't until I was getting ready for bed that it struck me that this was the night before Thanksgiving.

And in ninety days, we'd have no place to live. After the trouble we'd had finding this house, I knew that, while children aren't welcomed by landlords, dogs are generally forbidden. Sherman said his parents rented to us only because we'd be too grateful to complain about the shape the place was in—and they hadn't even known about our dogs.

Thanksgiving, I thought. Big deal, getting dressed up for company, some strange woman and her mother.

Then I remembered Laurelle saying, "Maybe she'll be a terrific person."

She could be, I thought. Irene Vardis could be a warm, kind, gentle woman. She might be as easy to like as Pat Troup, and I'd thought if Pat and my father got married, it would be okay, especially if they could afford to buy a house with their two salaries.

Irene Vardis probably earned far more than Pat did.

Irene Vardis might be somebody you would take to right away, honest and friendly and great with children. Her mother could be a wise, patient woman who would love to tell kids about the old days.

I wondered how they felt about dogs.

Ten

I think it was the smells that woke me Thanksgiving morning—onion and sage and melted butter.

I could hear the twins waking. After their first stirring, one of them always started talking, and then the other would answer in a groggy voice. It reminded me of fledgling birds greeting each other and the morning.

I kept my eyes shut. I didn't want to walk into the kitchen while the turkey was being stuffed.

The twins got up and dressed and left the bedroom, but I couldn't get back to sleep. I guess you never get so old that a holiday isn't a special event.

By now I was looking forward to meeting Irene Vardis and her mother.

After a time the twins came in. It is not easy to keep your eyes closed while five-year-olds stare at you, but I did, until Antony, his face inches from mine, announced that breakfast would be ready in five minutes.

Even my father managed to seem cheerful at breakfast.

After the dishes were done, Mrs. Farisee went to her room to iron the table linens. First, though, she told my father to put away all the books and papers he had piled up on the dining room table. She set the twins to tidying the parlor, and she had me get down all our dishes and glasses, except for the plastic ones, and check them over for chips and cracks and scratches.

I inspected the china and glasses, blew a few dog hairs off them, set the best on the counter, and put the rest back in the cupboard.

Mrs. Farisee came in looking like an Egyptian temple priest, with her arms held out before her, the table linens draped over them. I followed her into the dining room and helped her spread the cloth on the table, and set the napkins where the plates would go.

"Now," Mrs. Farisee told me, "I'll get on with the rest of the cooking, and you can finish setting the table. Put the carving set by my place. . . . I've seen what your father does trying to slice a roast. Antony, you help your sister. Aida, you take your bath now, and your brother will be next."

At least she didn't tell my father when to bathe.

I figured he would sit at one end of the table, with Mrs. Farisee at the other end. I'd seen enough movies to know that the guests should be at the right and left of my father.

I stacked all the dinner plates at Mrs. Farisee's place. With the twins at the table, if we passed around bowls and platters of food, we would be asking for trouble.

Our three good goblets I put where my father and the guests would sit.

We had only six salad plates. But since I wouldn't be eating turkey, I could put my salad on my dinner plate.

Placing forks and spoons and napkins very carefully, my brother was solemn and absorbed.

My father was on his knees before the parlor fireplace, using a dustpan to shove ashes and bits of burned wood onto newspapers he'd spread out on the hearth.

It struck me this Irene must be very neat, if he was even fussy about how the fireplace looked.

Being tidy was no crime.

I went on setting the table, but my mind wasn't on what I was doing. If my father was going to have trouble raising seven hundred dollars, he certainly wasn't going to have enough money for a down payment on a house in ninety days. But a woman who ran her own business could probably buy a place that would make this one look like a kennel.

Maybe she already had a house! If she ran a good-size company, she might have a big house. Maybe she'd been married before, and she was left in a home so huge she had her mother come live with her so she wouldn't rattle around in all the space.

It could be that her mother was just staying with her for a little while, and then Irene would have that enormous place, and nobody to share it with.

I went back into the kitchen. Mrs. Farisee was making a white sauce for the pearl onions.

"Do we have anything I could use to make place cards?" I asked.

"For seven people?"

"I thought it would be nice."

"Try your father," she suggested.

Aida tromped into the kitchen with her hair plastered to her skull. "Go dry your head," Mrs. Farisee told her, "and then you may put the marshmallows on the yams. Antony, bath time."

Before he could speak, she added, "And when you're finished, and *dry*, you may help fix the relish plate. Desdemona, you may put the candles and holders on."

This woman could run a government without any fuss at all, I thought. Somebody like Irene, with a big business, would probably give anything to have Mrs. Farisee look after her house.

After I set the tapers into the holders, I rearranged the silver and the napkins, feeling a little twinge at undoing my brother's work. But with the white tablecloth and the tapers in silver holders it wouldn't do to have the forks lying across the knives, and the bowls of the spoons hiding the tines of the forks.

In the parlor, my father was turning the Hide-A-Bed cushions over.

"They're just as worn on the other sides," I told him. "Mrs. Farisee already turned them. Have you got anything I could use to make place cards?"

"Place cards?"

"Yes."

"I suppose you could use the backs of my cards. You'd just have to leave them lying flat by the plates, though."

"That will do."

He gave me ten cards that read FAIRFIELD COUNTY MENTAL HEALTH SERVICES with *Mark Blank* in small print in the lower right-hand corners, and his office phone number in the left.

They were too small, really, but after being so firm about having place cards, I was committed. I took them back to the room I shared with the twins.

I wrote the names very carefully, hoping Irene Vardis wouldn't think the place cards looked childish.

But maybe she adored children and couldn't have any of her own. If she had any, she'd certainly bring them to Thanksgiving dinner—unless she was divorced, and they were spending the day with their father.

Better figure she has no kids, I thought. Keep it simple.

If the twins and I liked her right away, my father would be delighted. And if she heard the dogs barking and wanted to meet them, we'd know she was our kind of person.

When I finished the place cards, I brought them in to the kitchen and showed them to Mrs. Farisee. "You don't think these look like something a kid would do?" I asked her.

"They look fine," she assured me.

Aida came over and looked at them. "How about I draw a Thanksgiving picture to go with them?"

Mrs. Farisee tied a dish towel around my sister's neck, over her red velveteen dress, like a bib. "And I do not want to find one crayon mashed into the rug!"

Antony wandered in.

"Go to your room and dry your hair and button your shirt properly," Mrs. Farisee told him.

Arranging the place cards around the table took some thinking.

Aida was more likely to knock over her glass during a meal. On the other hand, Antony was apt to do something weird, like buttering his knuckles. I decided to put Antony next to Irene's mother. She probably wouldn't be so fast to get out of the way of spilled drinks.

Irene would be safest between my father and me. It wouldn't do to have her drenched with milk, or distracted by Antony trying to fill the holes in the olives with cranberry sauce.

After I arranged the place cards around the dining room table, I went back into the kitchen.

Mrs. Farisee was opening the jars and bottles and cans she had set out on the kitchen table—spiced peaches and bright red sweet spiced crab apples and black olives and two kinds of jam. I put them in bowls and then, while Antony arranged carrot and celery sticks and artichoke hearts and pickles on a platter, I filled the sugar bowl and set it by the cream pitcher and cups and saucers. Then I measured out the coffee and did the other odds and ends Mrs. Farisee thought of.

My father strolled in, shaved and showered and smelling of men's cologne. "Anything I can do to help?"

Mrs. Farisee and I glanced at each other. I could almost hear her thinking, *Men!*

My father looked at me as if he was having trouble getting used to his contact lenses again. "You have to pick up these people, do you?" I asked him.

"No. They'll take a cab over."

"Oh, good."

He went into the parlor, and I heard him turn on the radio and turn from station to station, finally stopping at a music program loaded with syrupy violins. I could not help but wince. Normally, my father's taste ran to Joe Cocker and Roy Orbison and B. B. King.

"Soft music. Easy listening. Songs to throw up by,"

I muttered. "If he starts buying gold chains to hang around his neck, I'm really going to worry."

"You go set out your clothes and be sure your sister's artwork is under control," Mrs. Farisee told me. "It will be a few minutes before there's enough hot water for your bath."

Aida's Thanksgiving picture had Pilgrims and turkeys and Indians and even a Christmas tree in it.

I owned three good winter dresses. I took out the newest, a purple knit. After all, it was a holiday and we were having company.

I heard the radio announcer introducing a Barry Manilow medley.

When I got out of the tub, I wiped the steam off the medicine cabinet and looked at myself.

My hair had grown out to a good two inches all over my head. With so many girls in school wanting a cut like mine, I'd stopped worrying about how short it was. But with somebody coming for dinner who might have a big house and love kids and dogs, and secretly loathe Easy Listening, I didn't want to look too much like a rebel.

After I dressed, I studied and admired Aida's picture and helped her wash crayon off her hands and quarry it from under her nails.

Mrs. Farisee had tidied the kitchen so that the only things sitting out were those we were going to use. On the wooden table were the coffee cups and saucers, the creamer and sugar bowl, the pumpkin pies covered by clean dish towels, and an assortment of serving dishes and utensils, including the grave-digging spoon, its handle slightly bowed.

Mrs. Farisee, in one of her good flowered polyester dresses and a fresh white apron, had opened the oven door and was shifting things around on the shelves.

The old kitchen, the woman peering into the oven of the ancient stove, the pies and serving dishes on the table, looked like the pictures of Thanksgiving you see on the calendars that drugstores give away free. And the smells—pumpkin, dressing, roast tur-key—were the smells from every Thanksgiving I could remember, every Thanksgiving I'd had with my mother and father. It all hit me, with no warning, and I hurried to the bathroom.

The dumbest things make you cry. I must have seen *Lassie Come Home* a dozen times, and I still start sniffling when Lassie does limp home.

I stood in the bathroom until I was sure I wasn't going to start sobbing again.

After I washed my face with cold water, I looked in the mirror. My eyes were bloodshot and my lids puffy.

I poured some of my father's after-shave on a washcloth and held it over my eyes.

You never want to put after-shave on your eyes.

I slapped my other hand over my mouth to muffle my yelp.

When I was able to see, I threw the washcloth in

the empty clothes hamper. Then I fished it out again. If Irene or her mother used the bathroom, I didn't want them to wonder why it reeked of after-shave.

I heard the dogs barking, and then there was a knock on the bathroom door. "You've been in there forever," Mrs. Farisee said, "and the company's here."

I opened the door.

"Oh, my word," she gasped. "What have you done to yourself?"

"I got after-shave in my eyes."

Mrs. Farisee shook her head. "Desdemona, why can't you just be an ordinary, maladjusted twelve-year-old?"

The dogs were still barking.

Mrs. Farisee opened the bathroom window. "QUIET!"

Even the dogs in the yard behind ours stopped barking. When Mrs. Farisee yelled "QUIET!" sometimes the whole street fell silent.

Our doorbell rang.

"I can't go in there looking as if I've been crying," I said.

"Who's going to be common enough to come out and ask?"

"But they'll wonder."

"They'll wonder more if you lurk in the bathroom until dinner." Holding my arm firmly, she led me in through the dining room to the parlor.

My father was just opening the front door. "Welcome," he said to the women who entered.

Why can't he just say "Hello"? I wondered. "Welcome" made him sound like Count Dracula greeting visitors to the castle.

The woman who'd come in first was not much over five feet tall, but she held herself very straight. Her hair was white and fine, and her face was thin, her skin dry and crackly as parchment, drawn tight across the bones. The pupils of her pale blue eyes were tiny, and her gaze was as sharp as a hawk's. She wore black pumps, sheer black stockings, a black coat of a wool so fine it looked almost like silk, black gloves, and a black hat.

The younger woman was a little taller than my father, and he stands five foot ten. Her hair was reddish brown, thick and straight, and cut so the front ends just cleared her jaw. Her eyes were a clear, light blue, her eye shadow was a faint brown, her lips a soft, glossy peach shade.

"Irene, Mrs. Vardis, I'd like you to meet . . ." He turned toward us, and his gaze fell on me. "Oh, good heavens."

"It's nothing," I assured him hastily. "Just a trivial."

"You mean trifle?" Even at a time like this, my father worried about words.

"Yes," I said. "Trifle."

He peered at me, blinking, and I could see he was having trouble with his near vision. "Are you sure you're all right, honey?" he asked.

I think Mrs. Farisee realized how embarrassed I

was. "Desdemona just got something in her eyes."

My father always figured that if Mrs. Farisee said something, it had to be so. He picked up from *Oh, good heavens.* "Irene, Mrs. Vardis, this is our housekeeper, Mrs. Farisee."

"I'm glad you could come," Mrs. Farisee said.

Irene Vardis didn't answer Mrs. Farisee, or even look right at her, but smiled a brief, icy little smile, as if she'd been greeted by a child she didn't want getting too friendly. Peeling off her gloves, she said to my father, "We had such a time getting a taxi. I had no idea it would be a problem on a holiday." She put her purse on the table by the door, and turned so my father could help her off with her coat.

Mrs. Vardis did not even smile. She handed Mrs. Farisee her purse and scarf, then carefully removed her hat, put it on top of the purse, and turned her back, waiting to be peeled out of her coat by our housekeeper.

Quickly, my father helped Mrs. Vardis shed her coat, then handed both wraps to me.

Mrs. Farisee turned to go.

"Here! I want my purse!" Irene's mother snatched her purse from under her hat.

I followed Mrs. Farisee into the hall. I was furious, and ashamed. She had spent days making a holiday dinner when she didn't have to, and my father's guests treated her like a hat rack.

"Dinner will be ready in twenty minutes." Mrs.

Farisee didn't let any feeling creep into her voice. She put the hat and scarf on the closet shelf and went into the kitchen.

I shoved our polished wooden hangers aside and hung the coats on two wire ones. I was about to go after Mrs. Farisee, but then I realized she probably wanted to be left alone.

When I walked back into the parlor, Mrs. Vardis was sitting like a judge in an overstuffed chair, while Irene and my father sat on the sofa, side by side. The twins stood, their backs to the window, watching Mrs. Vardis silently.

"I don't think I introduced my older daughter," my father said. "Mrs. Vardis, Irene, this is Desdemona."

Mrs. Vardis nodded.

Irene Vardis smiled and said, "Desdemona."

Her smile had all the warmth and sincerity of a beauty contestant's.

"Dinner will be ready in twenty minutes," I told my father.

"Would anyone like hot cider?" he asked.

"No, thank you," Mrs. Vardis murmured.

"Yes, I will," Irene said.

"Desdemona. Antony. Aida." My father left the room.

We followed.

In the hall, he murmured, "You're not behaving very well."

"Neither are those women," I said.

We walked into the kitchen.

"Dinner will be ready in fifteen minutes." Mrs. Farisee was brisk.

"Shall I pour you some hot cider?" he asked her.

"I can help myself," she said.

Using a platter as a tray, he managed to crowd five cups of cider on it, then shoved through the swinging door into the dining room. The twins followed him, barely missing being flattened by the door's return swing.

Mrs. Farisee got the turkey out of the oven without any help. While my sympathy was with the bird, I was worried for her as she hoisted it from the pan to the platter, almost dropping it on the floor.

Letting out a whoosh of relief, she stood with her arms braced on the table, her blue-tinted curls a little damp around her forehead. "It has to settle for a few minutes."

She had me put on the salads and the relish platters, and the rolls and jam and butter. She brought in the peas and the pearl onions and the mashed potatoes and gravy, muttering to me, "Quick! Quick! Quick! Get a trivet under it."

Back in the kitchen, she handed me a chilled bottle of sparkling cider wrapped in a dish towel. "Have your father pour, if he can see well enough. And tell them dinner's ready. Ask them to start the vegetables around so they don't get cold."

I set the cider on the table and said loudly to my father, "Dinner is ready."

"I want to freshen up," Mrs. Vardis announced.

My father didn't merely give her directions—he escorted her into the hall and right to the bathroom door.

I showed the twins their chairs, but I let Irene read the place cards.

When my father returned to the dining room, Antony and Aida and Irene Vardis and I were standing around the table.

"Mrs. Farisee said to start the vegetables around so they don't get cold." I knew we couldn't sit down until Mrs. Vardis returned, but I thought she could well have gone to "freshen up" before it was time to eat.

My father cast me a quick glance of reproach. Then he lit the candles, overshooting the wicks on the first two passes.

We stood, and stood. I watched the steam from the vegetables dwindle.

"Desdemona!" Mrs. Farisee called from the kitchen. "Hold the door."

I got up and held open the swinging door. Mrs. Farisee came through with the candied yams steaming in a casserole dish, a folded towel under it. She set it down on the towel—we'd run out of anything to use for a trivet. Then she looked around the table at the five of us standing, and the vegetables cooling.

Mrs. Vardis came through the parlor to the dining room, her step firm.

"Mrs. Vardis, why don't you sit here." My father hurried to pull out the chair on his right.

She didn't apologize for making us wait, she didn't smile at anybody, she just sat down.

Irene Vardis sat at my father's left, and the twins where I had told them.

I moved down to the other end of the table.

My father looked at me hard for just an instant, then he sat at the head of the table, and I took the chair at Mrs. Farisee's right.

"Well. I believe we're supposed to start." My father passed the rolls to Mrs. Vardis. "Everything looks wonderful, Mrs. Farisee." He passed the butter to Mrs. Vardis, then looked at Irene. "Doesn't it?"

She nodded. "It's so hard to get good help these days."

Mrs. Farisee strode back to the kitchen, hitting the swinging door so hard with her hand that I was afraid it would come right off the hinges.

"Excuse me." My father went after her. Sozzled with love he might be, but he was still conscious enough to see he had a rebellion brewing.

This was a time when the best thing for me to do was stay out of the way.

The guests and the twins and I sat there, not speaking. I could hear low but urgent voices in the kitchen.

Mrs. Vardis passed the rolls across to Irene, and then the butter. Irene took a roll and a pat of butter and passed the roll basket and the butter dish back to her mother. Neither of them so much as glanced at Aida, Antony, or me.

Both women broke their rolls and buttered them as if they were used to doing everything together.

Suddenly Aida spoke. "My brother almost drank rocks' eyes."

Mrs. Vardis and Irene looked at her blankly.

"If we had let him," Aida went on, "the rocks' eyes would have lit up all his insides. And then we would have had to take him to a hospital to have his stomach pumped out. I don't know how they pump your stomach out. Maybe up through your mouth. I don't know if all the insides attached to your stomach come out, too."

"All my insides?" Antony looked anxious.

"Oh, they have to put them back, or you'd die," Aida assured him. "They probably pump them back the same way they pumped them out. Anyway, you didn't drink the rocks' eyes."

Irene set her piece of roll down, untasted. So did her mother.

"Did Herb have his insides pumped out that time he threw up?" Antony stood up in his chair to reach the dish of cranberry sauce.

"Our dog Herb just started vomiting one night," Aida confided to Irene Vardis.

"First he threw up his dinner. It was a lot of brown chunks in a kind of gravy." Antony looked around for something to pour cranberry sauce into. "Then he threw up all this green slimy stuff, and then some yellow foamy goop that smelled weird. Our father *rushed* him right to the animal hospital, but he wouldn't bring us. When he came home, he said the doctor thought Herb might have a bone stuck in his bowel."

Irene Vardis and her mother sat like figures in a wax museum.

Leaning over, I put a dinner plate in front of my brother so he'd be free to go on talking. I was hoping my father and Mrs. Farisee wouldn't return too soon.

"Your intestines are your bowels," Aida informed Irene.

Antony looked puzzled. "Do bowels have bones in them?" He tilted the dish of cranberry sauce over his plate, and of course all the sauce slurped out.

"No, no." Aida was patient and a little overbearing. "The doctor meant Herb might have *swallowed* a bone." With the air of someone whose duty it is to inform and instruct, she turned to Mrs. Vardis again. "If you let your dog have bones, he can chew them up into big *splinters* that can clog up his intestines or even rip holes in them!"

Antony began to look uneasy again. "Then do they have to pump the dog's bowels out of him?" He lifted his plate to pour some of the cranberry sauce back into its serving dish.

To my disappointment, the kitchen door swung open, distracting him. My father held the door while

Mrs. Farisee stepped through, carrying the turkey on a platter. The great browned bird impressed Antony so much that he put down his plate.

Looking pale and queasy, Irene and her mother didn't show the slightest interest in the turkey.

Mrs. Farisee set the platter at her end of the table and sat down.

Irene and Mrs. Vardis glanced at her, then glanced at each other. It was plain they hadn't expected the help to actually eat with us.

Mrs. Farisee picked up the carving knife.

"I think that's the finest-looking turkey I've ever seen," my father pronounced.

"That's a turkey?" My sister's voice was small and tense.

"That's right," my father told her. "That's our Thanksgiving tur—" Then his glance fell on the cranberry sauce filling Antony's plate.

Aida's voice rose, shrill and horrified. *"Where's its face?"*

Mrs. Farisee looked at my father helplessly, then steadied the bird with the carving fork.

"Don't cut it!" my sister screamed.

My father hurried around the table and lifted her from her chair and carried her out of the room.

Antony stood up to get a better look at the turkey. His foot slipped and he lurched forward, his elbow landing on the edge of his plate, flipping it like a tiddlywink toward Irene Vardis.

She let out a kind of a muffled squeal, cranberries

in her hair, on her neck, cascading down the front of her dress.

Getting his feet firmly on the chair again, my brother cried out, shocked, "It *doesn't* have any head!"

Mrs. Farisee grabbed him.

I held the swinging door open for her, and then followed them.

In our room, my father sat Aida on her bed and Mrs. Farisee plunked Antony down on his.

"What did they do to it?" my sister wailed.

My father turned to me. "Did you . . ."

"No," I said. "She saw some live ducks and some pictures of live turkeys and made the connection herself."

"Aida . . ." My father sat on her bed.

"What happened to it?" she demanded.

"Was that a live turkey once?" Antony quavered.

"Desdemona, come along," Mrs. Farisee said.

I followed her to the kitchen. She started the coffee and sliced the pie. I felt so sorry for the twins that for a while I didn't even think about our guests in the dining room. When I did, I glanced at Mrs. Farisee, but neither of us went in to see how the women were doing. Maybe I just wanted to savor that glimpse of Irene Vardis decked with cranberry sauce.

After a few minutes, my father came into the kitchen. "Irene and her mother have been sitting in there alone all this time?"

Before Mrs. Farisee or I could answer, he hurried into the dining room.

Moments later, he opened the swinging door. "I'm going to run my guests home," he said stiffly. "They're feeling . . . a little fatigued."

After he'd left with his guests, Mrs. Farisee and I warmed up the rolls and vegetables.

"I am not going to have my Thanksgiving dinner with the turkey banished from the table," she declared.

The twins were watching a Peanuts Thanksgiving special on the television in our room. Neither of them glanced at me. I put their plates, loaded with everything except turkey, on the nightstand, along with two glasses of cider.

"Company barely touched anything," Mrs. Farisee observed, as she and I sat down at the dining room table.

"Hardly anything," I agreed.

She filled my glass with cider, and didn't even urge me to taste the turkey. The candles were burning low, but they lasted through the meal.

Mrs. Farisee didn't call the twins in to help with dishes. I suspect she decided that, so long as they were settled down, we should leave them alone.

She washed and I dried.

"I'm glad there's no school tomorrow," I said. "I couldn't stand it if somebody asked, 'How was your Thanksgiving?' "

For a minute, it almost looked as if Mrs. Farisee smiled.

"What if my father really cares about that Irene?" I wondered.

"There's no accounting."

"What if he wants to marry her?"

"I won't be around if he does. I would not put up with those women for five minutes."

My brother and sister trailed in. "May we have more pie?" Antony asked.

Mrs. Farisee got a pie out of the refrigerator.

"What does he *see* in Irene Vardis?" I persisted. "How can a man like my father be taken in by a person like that?"

"Blinded by passion," my sister murmured.

Mrs. Farisee eyed her narrowly. "Been watching soap operas secretly again, have we?"

I went to bed when the twins did. I didn't want to be awake when my father got home. What could I say to him?

It was not that easy getting to sleep. I wondered how I could have imagined a woman I'd never seen could be the answer to our problems.

But what if my father was mad about her? What if he was so in love, he'd marry her no matter what his children thought? What if he took us to live with that awful woman and her awful mother?

Would that be worse than having no place to live?

Eleven

Herb and Joe and Sadie and the twins woke me the next morning, standing by my bed, staring at me. "You missed breakfast," Antony announced.

When I wandered into the kitchen, Mrs. Farisee was making a turkey casserole.

"Your breakfast is in the warming oven," she greeted me.

I looked into the parlor. The Hide-A-Bed was made up, and my father's briefcase was gone.

"Did he go to work or house hunting?" I asked.

"He didn't say." She scattered bread crumbs over the top of the casserole. "Gone courting, more likely."

I finished eating and washed my dishes and got out of the kitchen before she could think of any chores for me.

I wondered how Sherman was doing, but it would probably seem odd if Mrs. Farisee called his house a second time to ask about him.

I dialed Laurelle's number.

She answered the phone herself.

"Listen," I told her, "I'm wondering how Sherman's doing, but I don't have the nerve to call his house. Would you . . ."

"Sure."

If it hadn't been for Sherman's posters, I thought, I might never have discovered what a neat person Laurelle was.

She called back in a few minutes. "He was able to talk to me himself. He has to stay in today, but he's sure he can come to the play, except he has no way to get there. So I asked my mom, and he's coming with us. You've got the fliers. . . ."

"They won't be ready until morning. There were a lot of orders ahead of ours. I'll pick them up and meet you guys at school by one-thirty."

"Okay. I'll get the programs from Razi and help you stick the fliers in until I have to go down to do makeup."

I was impressed. Once those fliers were discovered, she'd be a prime suspect. Not only that, here she was, one of the most popular girls in school, willing to be seen at the play with an eleven-year-old wimp.

Of course, she would not be the only suspect. The people who handed out those fliers would surely be questioned. I could only hope that the school wouldn't think putting fliers in programs was more serious than sharpening drumsticks.

Meanwhile, there was our family's future to worry

about. Could I let my father ruin all our lives, without putting up a fight?

Pat Troup was not listed in the telephone book.

The Information operator had a number for only one Troup—Eleazar.

I telephoned the newspaper. The operator who answered said Pat wasn't there.

"Could you give me her home number?" I asked.

"We are not allowed to," he said.

"This is kind of an emergency," I pressed.

"I'm sorry." He was firm. "It's newspaper policy. Could I put you through to another reporter?"

"No. It's . . . personal."

"She should be in Monday."

I knew what had to be done, and I didn't want to do it. But there was nobody but me, now, to look after my brother and sister and dogs.

I knocked twice on Eleazar Troup's front door.

He opened it and eyed me bleakly. "What?"

I reminded myself that my dogs and my family were at stake. "I wonder if I could have Pat's phone number."

"Why?"

"I need to talk to her. It's pretty urgent."

"Wait."

He shut the door, leaving me on the porch.

A minute later, I heard him. "Pat? That girl next door wants your telephone number. Says it's urgent. Shall I give it to her?"

Opening the door, he thrust a telephone at me, and shut the door on the cord.

"Dez?" Pat sounded concerned. "What's the problem?"

"I need to talk to you."

Pat didn't fool around. "You want to meet me at that health food restaurant on Tenth Avenue?"

"Yes," I said.

"Shall I come pick you up?"

"No," I said quickly. I could imagine my father coming home just as I was getting into her car. "I can be there in about twenty minutes."

"Fine."

I knocked on the door again, and when Mr. Troup opened it, I handed him his telephone. "Thank you. I hope the wire didn't get squashed."

Mrs. Farisee was standing on a chair in our kitchen, wiping down a cupboard shelf.

"I'm going over to Tenth Avenue to meet a friend," I told her.

She climbed down off the chair and rinsed the paper towel she was using—Mrs. Farisee wasted nothing. "Who?"

I had hoped she wouldn't ask. "Pat Troup."

She didn't ask why I was meeting Pat or try to talk me out of it. "Where on Tenth Avenue?"

"That health food place."

"Come directly home afterward."

It took me a little more than fifteen minutes to get to the health food restaurant. The menu was written in white chalk on a blackboard outside the door, and the windows weren't very clean, but the hanging plants looked healthy.

Pat was sitting at a table near the door, wearing a red U2 sweatshirt, a green and blue serape, and old brown tweed trousers tucked inside maroon nylon rain boots. The thick plastic lenses of her glasses were networked with tiny scratches, and the frames were not quite straight. But, I guess because she was so straight-on, she looked interesting rather than sloppy.

"How about a hot carob?" she greeted me. "I'll treat."

I didn't think she should buy me anything after I was the one who asked to meet her, but I wanted to get to what was on my mind, and I was afraid she'd keep suggesting things to drink.

"Okay. Thanks," I said.

She went to the counter and ordered, and as soon as she came back, I told her about the dogs running through the Groves' concrete, and about our being evicted.

She looked truly sorry. "That's terrible."

"And there's nothing we can do about it. With us gone, there'll be nobody but your dad left to keep the Groves from tearing down the whole block."

She smiled, but it looked as if the smile hurt her. "My father cut a deal with the Groves. He's trading his house for one of the condos they're building on Twelfth—and a piece of the action."

I was shocked. She'd written a three-part story for the paper about poor people being squeezed out of their homes by expensive condominiums. "Aren't those condos expensive?"

"Oh, yes. But it would cost the Groves even more to go through a legal battle with my dad. It would be terrible publicity for them, too, forcing an old man out of his home. They're buying his house for a whopping price, cash, and he's getting a condo for a small down payment and investing some of his cash in the condos they'll build on your block." She shook her head. "So there goes the neighborhood—truly."

A young man with a ponytail and one hoop earring brought our carob drinks.

Walking to the health food café, I'd wondered how I would dare talk about my father to the woman he'd dumped for Irene. Now I said, without even stopping to think, "I always figured that if anything developed between you and my father, say you got married, we'd all get along okay."

"That's not going to happen."

Since I'd already gone too far, I blurted out, "I don't know what happened between you and him, but if you want to get back together, I'll help."

She shook her head. "Oh, Dez."

"Wouldn't you even *want* to marry him?"

I half expected her to give me a sharp answer, or even to walk out. It was what I deserved. But she only said, "No."

154

She was my last chance, and without her there was nothing to hope for. "Are you sure?"

She nodded. "I've *been* married. Once is enough."

My father went out Friday night. I didn't ask him where. I knew someday, before it was too late, I'd have to tell him how I felt about Irene Vardis, but I thought I'd better do it when the play was over—and when he'd had plenty of time to recover from Thanksgiving dinner.

Twelve

The next morning after breakfast, my father said, "I have some things to attend to. I won't be home until noon."

"Could you make it a little earlier? I have to . . ." If I said I had to pick something up, he might offer to do it for me on his way home. ". . . get ready."

"We'll be at the play in plenty of time, honey."

I didn't ask him if he was going to go house hunting, or if he'd been house hunting. If he said no, that would mean he wasn't worried.

He should have been worried. He had had a horrible time finding this place. No man with three children and three dogs is likely to turn up many people willing to rent him a house.

If my father wasn't worried, it could mean he already had a place in mind.

The only place I could think of would be Irene Vardis's house.

Maybe she wouldn't even let him bring the dogs.

No, I told myself. He would never give up the dogs.

But what if he had no other way to get a home for himself and his children?

And I was about to bring down the wrath of the school on myself and make even more problems for him. "You don't really have to come to the play," I told him.

"Sure I do. How often does my own kid make posters for a play?"

"I have to get there by one-thirty to hand out programs."

"Fine. I'll drop you there and then come back about a quarter past two."

I could think of no way to talk him out of it. He'd even invited Mrs. Farisee. But she said that, though she had done many reckless things in her life, she was not about to try sitting through a play with two five-year-olds.

My father left, after telling me all the things he always did when he left me home—don't open the door for anyone, don't go anywhere, keep the twins in and under control.

I felt so guilty not telling him about the fliers that I was tempted to go after him and confess. But that would be finking on Sherman and Laurelle. Besides, though I respected my father, you can't be all that sure about how an adult is going to react. What if he ordered me not to have anything to do with the fliers? I figured I would tell him when it was all over.

Of course, by Monday the school might be calling him in for a conference.

So I let him go, not asking him any questions or telling him anything that might upset him.

Sherman called at nine. "Everything's set, right?"

"How are you feeling?"

"Okay."

"You're sure?"

"I'm fine, Dez."

"You know my father's coming, with the twins."

"You're not going to tell him beforehand about the fliers?"

"No. I want to be sure I get there to help hand them out. I'll pick up the copies about noon—they couldn't do them any sooner."

"So we'll meet you there at one-thirty." He was quiet a minute. "Are you scared?"

"I think I'm even more scared than when we took the ducks, Sherman."

At ten-thirty, I sent Aida in to bathe.

By noon, the twins and I were all bathed and dressed and I had lunch on the table. I felt as if I'd like to go lie down with my feet up for the rest of my life.

"You've got your shoes on the wrong feet," my sister told my brother.

"Do not," he said.

"You look as if you're walking around a corner," I said. I made him put his shoes on the right feet and helped him tie his laces.

I got that line from Sherman. According to him, Estes Kefauver, who ran for President of the United States in 1956 but didn't get the nomination, was so absentminded he sometimes wore his shoes on the wrong feet. And he was so stubborn he'd insist they were on the right feet. It was his wife who told a reporter that Estes sometimes looked as if he were walking around a corner.

I wonder if there is anybody in the United States except Sherman Grove who remembers that about Estes Kefauver.

I wonder if there is anybody but Sherman who remembers Estes Kefauver.

Sherman is not the salt of the earth. Sherman is the nutmeg.

At twelve-fifteen, my father showed up. I was furious with him for being so late, but of course I couldn't let him know why it mattered so much.

"I already ate," I told him. "I have to go out for a little while."

"We'll have to leave here right after one if I'm supposed to get you there in time," he protested.

"I'm all dressed. I'll be home by one-fifteen. This is important."

"No later," he warned.

The copy shop was crowded, with three people behind the counter looking frazzled as they tried to wait on everybody.

Edging forward little by little, I finally stood at the counter with customers on either side of me.

The clock on the wall at my right said one.

Being a kid means that adults get waited on ahead of you, no matter whose turn it is.

Finally, though, I said to a clerk, "Excuse me. I'm here for my order."

"Name?" she asked.

"Blank," I said.

She looked impatient. *"Name."*

"My name is Blank," I told her, wishing I'd said something like Smith or Jones when I brought the fliers in. "Desdemona Blank."

"I'm in a hurry," the man on my right interrupted.

"Name?" she asked him.

"Club Manhattan," he said.

She got all sniffy about Blank, I thought, but she doesn't even blink at a man named Club Manhattan. Then I realized that was probably the name of a business, not a person.

As the clerk started for the back room, the woman on my right called, "Can you get mine while you're at it? Owens."

It was one-fifteen.

I got out my money, while the other clerks set packages down on the counter and rang up sales or wrote out charge-account bills.

Our clerk came back and set three packages on the counter. Then she took the slips of paper off each and went to the cash register. "Club Manhattan?"

"Bill me," the man said.

"You have an account?" she asked.

"Of course," he snapped.

She wrote on a pad, and he signed it, and she handed him one of the packages. Then she called out, "Owens," and took the woman's money and gave her a package.

I put my eighteen dollars and sixty cents on the counter. "Blank." I picked up the third package and hurried out while the clerk was still counting the money.

It was one thirty-five when I got home. I could tell my father was annoyed, but he didn't say anything.

When we started to the car, he glanced at the package I was carrying, but he was too irritated to ask questions. I was prepared to tell him the package was just something for the play, which was the truth, but not the whole truth, so I was relieved that he didn't mention it.

It's odd. I was terrified of what I was going to do, but I couldn't wait to get it over with.

There were only a dozen other cars parked by the junior high when we pulled up. "There's no point in going anywhere else now," my father said. "We'll come in with you."

"But I won't have time to hang out with you," I protested. "I'll have to help with . . . things."

He had got his good humor back. I suppose he'd had time to think that he'd been late home, too. "That's all right. We can look at the posters until it's time to find seats."

Sherman and Laurelle were inside the front door, with a woman and a girl of about sixteen.

"We were held up," I explained.

Our principal, Ms. Cohen, and a few teachers were standing in front of the auditorium's center front doors. Off to one side, Mr. Razi was talking to Elliot and a half dozen other kids. Ellliot glanced over at me, but he didn't even nod.

"How are you doing?" my father asked Sherman.

"Um . . . fine, sir." Sherman's voice was so small I could barely hear him.

I remembered the gift certificate back on my dresser. Just as well, I thought. It would feel strange to hand it to Sherman in public.

Mr. Razi had finished talking to the group. He clapped Elliot on the shoulder and hurried away.

"This is my mother and my sister Nicole," Laurelle said, clutching a package that looked as if it had been opened and then hastily closed again.

Mrs. Carson was a little under medium height, not overweight, but not thin. Her hair was short and blonde and curly, her eyes were gray, and her eyeshadow was bright blue. She didn't look cheap or anything. It's just that you don't often see blue eyeshadow on women any more. She wore a blue coat, with a blue suit under it, and a flowered silky blouse that tied at the neck. It was hard for me to tell how old she was. She just looked about the right age to be Laurelle's mother.

Nicole, Laurelle's sister, was gorgeous, with long,

wavy black hair and slate-colored eyes with long black lashes. She was taller than her mother, and thinner, and she acted as if it was all she could do to endure this afternoon.

I introduced my father and the twins to them, and then Laurelle grabbed my sleeve. "Could you come with me while I . . . attend to something? Mom, I probably won't see you until the play starts at least." She looked at my sister. "How would you like to help?"

Before I could say anything, she took Aida by the hand and started walking away.

"We may be gone a while," I told my father.

Sherman and I hurried after Laurelle and Aida.

As soon as we were out of earshot, Laurelle whispered, "Your father looks *nice*. Try to be sure he sits next to my mom."

"Okay. But . . ." I nodded toward my sister.

"We need her." Laurelle led us to the girls' bathroom. "Okay, Sherman, you have to warn us if anybody comes along while we're in there."

Sherman looked shocked.

"Whistle or something," she told him. "There's no other place open where we can work. And we can't have anybody come in and see what we're doing."

Leaving Sherman outside, we hurried into the rest room. "You were so late!" Laurelle opened the package. "I'm supposed to be on makeup right now. And, look. The school's copy people didn't even fold the programs, or put the covers on them, or staple them.

What we've got is a few hundred sheets of programs, and a few hundred blank cover sheets. And the audience is going to start coming any minute. You and I will have to put a blue sheet over each program and fold them, and your sister will have to fold a flier sheet and stick it in the middle."

I led Aida into a stall. "Sit down."

"But I don't have to . . ."

"No, no, no. Sit on the floor."

She looked shocked. "In here? In my good dress?"

"Aida, this is an emergency. Trust me. Believe me." I pressed down on her shoulder so she had to sit. Then I plopped the package of fliers face down on the floor beside her and tore off the wrapping. "You fold each sheet crossways. We will pass you some programs under your door, and you stick one of your folded sheets in the middle of each program. Got it?"

"Why do I have to stay in here?"

"So nobody can see what you're doing."

"But I'm just folding paper."

"Aida, don't argue. Just start folding, and I promise I will never tell Mrs. Farisee that you and Antony watch 'Creature Features' with the sound off when you're supposed to be asleep."

I left my poor sister in the stall and went to sit on the floor in front of the sinks, facing the door in case Sherman let anybody get by.

Laurelle had already put together and folded some programs. Now we worked assembly-line fashion. She slapped a blue sheet over a program sheet, and I folded it. When we had a pile of them, I shoved them under the door into the stall where my sister was working.

"They don't have any clothes on," she said through the door.

"Aida, don't start being silly. Animals are not supposed to have clothes on."

"We won't put fliers in the ones we give your family and mine and the teachers," Laurelle said. "That way, we'll at least get through the play before it all comes down on us."

It was a very small compromise, in the light of all the risk we were taking. I was all for it.

We'd folded a few dozen programs, keeping aside twenty and shoving the rest in for Aida to fill, when there was a knock on the door and Sherman's voice. "Oh, boy. We've got trouble!"

Scrambling to my feet, I hurried to Aida's stall. "Whatever happens," I rasped, "stay in there with those fliers, and don't make a sound!"

I heard voices outside, and then the door from the corridor opened. Ms. Cohen stood there, Sherman beside her looking scared.

"Laurelle Carson!" Ms. Cohen strode in. "You are supposed to be down there on makeup!"

Laurelle got to her feet. "I was just helping . . ."

"You help where you're supposed to be helping!" Ms. Cohen told her sternly. "Move!"

Laurelle looked at me helplessly and then walked out the door, Ms. Cohen right behind her.

I went on slapping covers on programs, folding them, sliding them under the door to my sister, and taking the ones she'd finished.

There was a knock on the door to the corridor. "Dez?" It was Sherman's voice. "Some people are showing up for the play."

I grabbed the programs without fliers in one hand and the pile Aida had finished in the other, and shoved the door open. "Be sure my family and Laurelle's and the teachers get *these,* and everybody else gets *these.*"

He took the first group in his right hand, the second in his left. "How am I supposed to do that?"

"You will have to carefully distribute the first ones, because they don't have fliers. *Then* everybody else gets the ones with fliers. By the time you get back, we'll have more done."

He took the programs, and I went back to work.

Aida's voice came from inside the stall. "Why do they have on just collars and bow ties and teeny underpants?"

I didn't stop working. "Who?"

"The men on the papers I'm supposed to fold."

As I yanked open the stall door, she held up a flier obligingly.

At the top of the page was printed in large letters, "Now! Straight from Las Vegas! Live! Appearing at Club Manhattan! Live! Male Exotic Dancers! The Ultimate in Striptease!" Under the printing were pictures of three young, muscular men wearing only little white collars and bow ties and tiny bikini underpants.

I didn't even bother to read the dates and prices at the bottom of the page. "Aida, stay there! Don't move! *Keep your stall door locked until I come back!*"

Sherman was inside the school's front door, just handing programs to a man and woman.

"Excuse me!" I snatched the programs from their hands. "There's been a . . . change."

Grabbing Sherman's arm, I pulled him away from the door.

"Are you crazy?" he gasped.

Elliot hurried to us. "What are you doing, grabbing those away from people?"

"I picked up the wrong fliers at the copy shop! What we put in the programs are advertisements for male striptease dancers!"

With a groan, Elliot started away.

"Wait!" Sherman ran after him. "Don't try to take programs away from any teachers. It would only alert them. And we didn't put any fliers in theirs."

Sherman and Elliot dashed into the right-hand doors to the auditorium. I ran in the left.

"Excuse me." I moved an usher aside and took the programs from the hands of the man and woman and little girl he was showing to their seats. "Wrong ones! Sorry!"

The usher said, "Hey!" but nobody tried to physically resist me.

At the other side of the auditorium, Sherman and Elliot were seizing programs from people.

I leaned over a woman sitting in the back row who was just opening her program. "Sorry. There's been a mistake. We'll bring you another one." I pried it from her grip and hurried on.

Half a dozen rows ahead, a group of three adults and two children was just getting settled. "Would you please give me back your programs?" I said. "We'll bring you the right ones." To my relief, they handed the programs down to me.

As I walked toward the front of the auditorium, scanning the seats for anybody that was not a teacher, I saw my brother in the third seat of the third row from the front, turning around, looking for me. My father was next to him, and Mrs. Carson on the other side of my father, with Nicole next to her. They had saved the two seats nearest the aisle.

The minute Antony saw me, he stood up and waved. I smiled, but didn't go any closer.

There were no other people sitting on my side of the auditorium.

I hurried toward the back, and the doors.

Sherman and Elliot were just coming out the other doors, clutching programs.

"Are you sure you got them all?" I took the programs Elliot was holding.

Sherman nodded.

Mr. Obledo, our math teacher, came out of the auditorium. "What is going on here?"

One of the ushers hurried over. "There are people coming in, and these guys are taking away programs instead of giving them out!"

"They were . . . they're not right," I stammered.

"Can you fix them?" Mr. Obledo demanded impatiently. "Right now?"

"Oh, yes. In practically no time." I grabbed Sherman by the arm.

Outside the girls' rest room, I took the stack of programs he held. "Keep watch! I'll get rid of the fliers." As I stepped into the rest room, I called, "Are you okay, Aida?"

"How long do I have to stay in here?" she quavered.

"Just give me time to think." I sat on the floor and pulled the fliers out of the programs we'd taken back.

When I stepped into the hall, Sherman said, "Dez, it's two-twenty."

I handed him the stack of programs. "Okay. Get the ushers to help you hand them out to everybody who doesn't have one."

He hurried away, and I went back into the bathroom.

My sister's voice was small and heart-wrenching. "Dez, this floor is cold."

No matter what she does in the future, no matter if she is a royal pain in the neck as a teenager, I will always remember how I left her, at five, sitting on the floor of a bathroom stall in her good dress with a stack of fliers for Club Manhattan.

I picked up the fliers beside her. I picked up those I'd taken from the programs. Then I just stood there in the girls' rest room, holding hundreds of ads for male striptease dancers.

If I dumped them in the trash bin, and the custodian saw them when he emptied it, there would be an investigation. The way things had been going for me lately, I could be sure that somehow the fliers would be traced to me.

Besides, I could not bring myself to dump hundreds of striptease advertisements in the bin where any junior high girl might see them. It could upset a sensitive kid. Or another kid might take one home to show her parents.

I fished through the trash bin. The paper wrappings Laurelle and I had torn off the programs and the ads were in pieces, but I found the heavy rubber bands that had been around my package.

I slipped the rubber bands around the fliers crossways and lengthways. Then I put on my coat and shoved the fliers under it, holding them against my stomach with my left arm.

I took my sister by the hand. "Whatever happens, whatever happens," I told her fiercely, "don't you breathe a word about those fliers or what we were doing in here! You promise!"

So, on top of everything I'd put her through, I terrified her into promising not to talk about it.

When I saw Ms. Cohen standing like a sentinel outside the doors to the auditorium, I almost turned back to the rest room. But she had spotted me.

There was nobody else in sight. I realized the play must have started.

As I stood, clutching the fliers against me, Ms. Cohen motioned us to her.

All I could do was obey.

When we got closer, she whispered, "What in the world have you been doing? I sent everybody else in five minutes ago. You'll have to sit in the first seats you find toward the back, and don't you dare make a *sound*."

The second to the back row was empty. I sat there with the fliers in my lap, trying to concentrate on the play, hoping my father wasn't worried about Aida and me.

Lars wore a turban, a lot of eyeliner, and a white polyester shirt with a short red sleeveless jacket. He had on blue pantyhose under bright green tight pants that reached just below his knees, and what looked like ballet slippers. I could imagine the kids on the costume committee ransacking their mothers' closets.

He forgot one of his lines right away, and you could hear somebody prompting him from the front row. Then his voice cracked while he was singing his first song. Still, you have to admire somebody who had the courage to come out on stage looking the way he did in front of people he knew.

Teena wore a high-necked, long-sleeved rust color blouse and a long, full black skirt that looked like velvet. She remembered most of her lines, so far as I could tell. But then, I wasn't listening that hard. Could we be absolutely sure we had retrieved every program with a flier in it? What if someone had gotten a program and then gone outside to wait for friends, or to get something out of a car?

When intermission came, I led Aida toward the front of the auditorium, against the tide of people coming out. I figured that the sooner my father saw us, the fewer questions he'd have.

As the crowd in the aisles thinned, I saw him standing, looking around him. Seeing me, he bent down to say something to Laurelle's mother. As Aida and I came closer, he nudged Antony out into the aisle, then held him back so Mrs. Carson and Nicole could pass.

The twins greeted each other as if they'd been separated for years. "Where were you?" my brother demanded.

Aida glanced up at me.

"Busy," I said.

We followed Laurelle's mother and sister out into the main hall.

"Handsome poster, Dez." My father nodded at the one on the wall to our right, but he didn't make any move to go look at the others.

"Well." Mrs. Carson looked around her. "It's a . . . a charming play."

"They've really tackled it with a lot of . . . enthusiasm," my father said.

Nicole looked straight ahead, not focusing on a single living person, like someone who is trying to survive in a crowded prison yard. Without a word, she made it clear that she was spending Saturday afternoon with her mother in public at a great personal sacrifice, and against her will.

My father and Mrs. Carson went on talking to each other.

I looked around at the other people in the lobby, most of them in pairs and groups, talking, some of them very animated. Anybody who had gotten a male striptease flier would surely be more than animated, I told myself.

Laurelle wormed through the crowd toward us, followed by Sherman.

"Hi," she said.

"Very good makeup, sweetie," her mother said.

"Very convincing," my father agreed.

"Thank you." Laurelle turned to me. "Could I speak to you a minute, Des?"

There were people going into the girls' rest room, so Sherman and Laurelle and I walked down to the end of the corridor.

I leaned against the wall. "I picked up the wrong fliers . . . hundreds of ads for . . ."

"Sherman told me. What did you do with them?"

I pointed at my stomach. "Under my coat."

"Oh, boy. We'll have to take them back Monday."

I hadn't thought of that. "I would never have the nerve! I would be embarrassed to death."

"Yeah, but they belong to somebody," Sherman reminded me.

"But we paid for them," I countered.

Laurelle managed to stay reasonable. "Dez, whoever got ours probably returned them. We can't get ours without giving these back, or without paying for ours a second time."

I had been through too much to worry about being reasonable. "I don't want to think about it tonight. I'm not sure how I'm ever going to live through this."

"Remember, the play just lasts an hour," she told me. "Keep reminding yourself you're halfway there."

"I'm halfway there, and I'm carrying hundreds of ads. . . ."

"Try to put that out of your mind." She took me by the arm.

I pulled away. *"Not that arm!* Do you want me dropping pictures of male strippers all over the corridor?"

When we got back to our families, my father and Mrs. Carson were talking about music—Brahms and Mozart. Nicole did not seem to have moved or changed her expression.

I was a little surprised that Sherman stayed with us. Considering that his parents were evicting my family, I would have expected him to be uncomfortable near my father. Of course, Sherman had always hung around my house in preference to his own.

Then I realized what was holding him. Every few seconds, his glance flickered over to Nicole, and then away.

Sherman, I thought, *she is sixteen if she's a day, and as warm and friendly as an ice cave.*

Ms. Cohen and some of the teachers started politely urging people into the auditorium. My father got us all settled in the third row, and again he sat next to Mrs. Carson.

He certainly seemed interested in her. Was he just plain fickle? Would he ever settle down? Or had Thanksgiving dinner with our family been more than Irene Vardis could handle? Had he been dumped again, this time thanks to his children?

I guess I heard and saw the rest of the performance, but I don't remember much of it. Something especially loud or interesting would take place on stage and seize my attention, but then my thoughts would return to my own life.

What if my father started dating Laurelle's mother? I wasn't sure how I'd feel about him going out with the mother of a friend of mine. Strange, that was for sure. On the other hand, I should be grateful for anybody who would keep him away from Irene Vardis.

That blue eyeshadow was really out-of-date. Then it occurred to me that maybe Mrs. Carson wore it because she was insecure about her looks. And for the first time, I wondered how she must be feeling. Losing her boyfriend and having her husband remarry, she was probably pleased to have a nice man treat her like an attractive, interesting person.

The applause startled me into paying attention. My father helped Mrs. Carson into her coat.

When we got outside, she put her arm around Laurelle's shoulder. "Would you all like to go get something to drink?" She looked at my father.

"I'm sure the kids would love to," he said. "Shall we follow you in our car?"

Trying not to grin, Laurelle glanced at me.

Instead of going right to our car, my father walked a way with Mrs. Carson. "Actually, it's so close to dinnertime . . ." he said.

Laurelle's mother stopped. "It is, isn't it?"

"I know a good Chinese restaurant. Desdemona's a vegetarian."

He said it as if it was a fact, not a problem. Right then I would have forgiven him if he'd been half an hour late to lunch.

Mrs. Carson nodded. "So is Laurelle. Chinese should be perfect for them."

Mrs. Carson and her daughters followed us in their car. My father parked halfway down the block from the restaurant, to leave a closer space for them.

It was so early we were the only customers. The waiters shoved two tables together for us. Anybody just looking would take us for a family, I thought.

"Don't you want to take your coat off?" my father asked me.

"No, thanks." I folded my hands in my lap.

He looked a little worried. "You're not coming down with a chill, are you?"

"Oh, no. I feel fine."

After we ordered, my father and Mrs. Carson got to talking about movies, and Laurelle kept glancing at me like a conspirator, trying not to grin. Nicole looked as if she had been seated at this booth by accident and forced to endure the company of strangers. Sherman was speechless, gazing at Nicole as if he couldn't help himself.

And I was sitting there with hundreds of ads for male striptease dancers in my lap. Laurelle and Sherman were good, true friends, but did they have any idea of the strain I was under?

Suddenly it occurred to me that while I was sitting there with hundreds of sleazy ads, somewhere in this town somebody, maybe the man from Club Manhattan who had ordered them, found himself with three hundred and fifty vegetarian fliers on his hands.

In spite of everything I'd gone through, in spite of all I was going through, I couldn't help wondering what that person was thinking.

The twins were the only people at our table interested in discussing *The King and I*. They got into wondering how people who wore hoop skirts could play baseball and drive cars. Demonstrating how a person would have to back into the driver's seat sideways, Aida knocked my tea over.

While my father blotted Aida and Antony, Mrs.

Carson took a sheaf of paper napkins out of the holder and mopped up the table as if overturning drinks was just something one should expect a five-year-old to do.

We left the restaurant, Nicole stalking ahead of the rest of us as if she were ignoring an unsavory group trying to strike up an acquaintance with her.

I lagged behind a little with Sherman and Laurelle. "Your mother's neat," I observed.

"Yeah."

I shifted the fliers to a more comfortable position. "Does she like dogs?"

"She loves them," Laurelle said. "She's always talking about the Airedale she grew up with. But we lived in apartments until a year ago. My folks broke up right after we bought our house. Getting a dog just never came up."

"Who got the house?" I didn't want to be pushy, but there was no telling what might develop between my father and Mrs. Carson.

"My mom."

What are you thinking? I asked myself. He has just met this woman. Besides, imagine living with Nicole! Of course, with her personality, she would probably move out on her own the minute she turned eighteen. And there was no harm just finding out a few basic facts.

"How many bedrooms?" I asked.

* * *

When we got home, the twins went to our room to change their clothes. I stayed in the parlor with my father.

"I have to talk to you." I sat beside him on the sofa. "I told you that Sherman was supposed to help me make play posters. Instead he made turkey posters."

"*Turkey* posters?"

"Posters about not eating turkeys." I told him about Sherman's visit to the turkey farm when he was little. "And . . . I don't know . . . it got Laurelle and me to thinking just how weird it is that we raise animals and then kill them and eat them. Suppose super beings came down from space, as advanced compared to us as we are compared to other animals. But suppose these advanced beings started caging us and slaughtering and eating us. Would they have a right to because they were so much smarter?"

"I see your point, but what are you getting at?"

"We did the play posters on the backs of the turkey posters and put up them up where both sides would show. You may run into one around town. But then we started thinking how measly eight posters were, and how there were a lot of animals—more than just turkeys—suffering every minute of their lives and killed for food. So what we did . . ." I hesitated. "We made up fliers about how food animals live and die, and asking people not to eat meat for Christmas. We planned to put them in the play programs."

"There was none in mine."

This was the hardest part yet. "We didn't put any in yours or Laurelle's family's. We didn't want to . . . I guess we didn't want to upset you until it was over."

"Wouldn't it have been simpler and more honest to tell us beforehand what you were going to do, instead of hiding it from us?" He was calm and serious, which made me feel much worse.

"We thought you'd tell us not to do it."

He nodded. "Mmm."

"Would you have?" I pressed.

"Probably."

"So I'm telling you now."

"It's not the same. I assume you didn't tell anybody at school what you were going to do either. Did you think about the repercussions?"

"Oh, yes. We figured we were going to get in trouble."

He looked at me in surprise. "But you went ahead."

"Martin Luther King said that you have to be ready to put your body on the line."

He came close to smiling. "So you'll go to school Monday and take whatever happens."

"Well, actually, I don't think anything will happen." This was downright embarrassing to admit.

"You don't think the school administration is going to be upset that you sneaked your own material into their programs without permission? Stop chewing your fingernails."

"I took the flier to be copied, and when I went back to the copy shop, I picked up the wrong package. So what we put in the programs were ads for a male exotic dance group."

That jolted him right out of being calm and reasonable. He planted his elbow on the arm of the sofa and rested his forehead on the heel of his hand.

"But we got all the programs back and took out the fliers before anybody saw them." I had been thinking of telling him about the ducknapping, to clear my conscience completely, but I could see that he wasn't up to dealing with any more confidences. "So somebody . . . probably somebody from Club Manhattan . . . has our vegetarian fliers, and I have hundreds of their ads."

He lifted his head. "*You* have them?"

"I had them under my coat all through the play and dinner," I burst out, relieved that I could at least give him an idea of what I'd gone through. "They're in the kitchen cupboard now. Laurelle says we have to return them."

"They're not your property." He had recovered enough to be cool and rational again.

"I would die. The men have on . . . little underpants and bow ties . . . but if I return them, the people at the copy shop will know that I *looked* at them."

"Then it's Club Manhattan who should be embarrassed. But they never intended to put that junk into your hands. So, tacky as the ads are, you'll have to take them back to the copy shop if you want your own fliers back."

"What if whoever has ours didn't return them?"

"You have the copy shop notify them that there's been a mixup. Then if they don't return your fliers, we will toss theirs into the trash."

I nodded. "Even if we get ours back, it's too late now."

"No, it's not. You just have to figure some acceptable way to distribute them."

"You're right." I was already thinking of the Mona Lisa, and the shoe repair shop, and the woman in the thrift shop. There had to be even more people in this town who would be willing to help distribute some vegetarian information.

I sat there with him for a minute, feeling better than I had all day.

"I'll have to hand out programs at the play tomorrow, too."

"Just plain programs, with nothing added."

"Right. But after all we went through volunteering, we've got to go back." It occurred to me that the minute Elliot or Mr. Obledo saw us, they might tell us to go away.

"Makes sense." He kissed my forehead. "And I want those Club Manhattan fliers out of the cupboard before Mrs. Farisee comes home tomorrow evening."

I went back to the bedroom to change.

182

"No," I told the twins. "No. I promised not to tell about 'Creature Features,' but I am not going to keep quiet while you watch 'The Beast with Five Fingers.' "

They knew I was serious. They turned up the sound and flipped through channels, arguing about programs.

Then I heard it.

It wasn't loud, but it was unmistakable.

In the parlor, my father was laughing.

We had to be out of our house in ninety days. Thanksgiving dinner with his Irene had been a disaster.

But at least the mess with the fliers had made somebody laugh.

And then I thought, *Wait a minute. If he can laugh, it's going to be all right.*

When my mother walked out on us, it was much worse than now. We were all in shock. But he pulled out of it. We moved to a new town, he got work, and he found us a house to live in.

It's his job to take care of us, and he's never failed us yet, I thought. *If he can laugh like this, with all he has on his mind, the least I can do is trust him.*

Nevertheless, in the morning I'd call Laurelle and see what her mom thought of him.